BROKEN THINGS
A Tale of Durstan

To, Dave

BROKEN THINGS
A Tale of Durstan

We are all broken things...

George Mann

Broken Things
A Tale of Durstan
Copyright George Mann © 2020

Cover Art
Copyright Daniele Serra © 2020

Introduction
Copyright Marie O'Regan © 2020

This hardcover edition is published in December 2020 by Absinthe Books, an imprint of PS Publishing Ltd, by arrangement with the author. All rights reserved by the author.

The right of George Mann to be identified as Author of this Work has been asserted by him in accordance with the Copyright, Designs & Patents Act 1988.

This book is a work of fiction. Names, characters, places and incidents either are products of the author's imagination or are used fictitiously. Any resemblance to actual events or locales or persons, living or dead, is entirely coincidental.

ISBN
978-1-786366-94-8
978-1-786366-95-5 (signed edition)

Design & Layout by Michael Smith
Printed and bound in England by TJ Books Limited

Absinthe Books
PS Publishing | Grosvenor House
1 New Road Hornsea, HU18 1PG | United Kingdom

editor@pspublishing.co.uk | www.pspublishing.co.uk

Introduction

WHEN I WAS ASKED TO HEAD ABSINTHE BOOKS by the wonderful Pete and Nicky Crowther of PS Publishing, I couldn't quite believe my luck. I was asked to find three authors for the first year's batch of novellas, and it wasn't hard to draw up a wish list

George Mann was an obvious choice for me. A very talented writer, both of novels and short stories—as well as an anthology editor. He is the author of the supernatural crime *Wychwood* series of novels, and the Victorian fantasy mystery *Newbury and Hobbes* novel series. He has also written in the Sherlock Holmes, *Star Wars* and *Doctor Who* franchises, to name just a few. George has very kindly written stories for me twice before: the hugely affecting 'Restoration' in my ghost story anthology *Phantoms* (2018, Titan Books), and the poignant 'About Time' in *Wonderland* (2019, Titan Books), co-edited with Paul Kane. I couldn't wait to see what he'd come up with at novella length, where his only restriction was that the tale had to have a speculative element, be that science fiction, fantasy, or horror.

Marie O'Regan

Broken Things is a fantasy novella, but edges into horror territory, in my opinion, with a decidedly dark tone. It also introduces the world of Durstan, a world of tree gods and magic, of knights and quests and honour. I sincerely hope George explores this further in the future. Amaranth has risen once again, and Nok must travel with her brother's bones on a quest to find the Queen of the Broken, as must Brother Ambrose and his scribe; Pallor, and his squire, the sarcastic Stonn. Each has their own desire, their own question for Amaranth… and each will find an answer, of a sort.

.

—Marie O'Regan
Derbyshire, 2020

BROKEN THINGS
A Tale of Durstan

For Michael Rowley.

Chapter One

And Lo! The Kith did rise,
From foetid swamp and gloom-ridden marsh,
To walk the lands of Wol.
How the dead did wail,
From their sunken groves and leafy burrows,
As the Children of the Elk,
With sickle-hands,
Did reap a bitter harvest.

The Quietus Codex, attribution unknown

THE FIRST THAT NOK KNEW OF THE HOMUNCULUS was not the light pitter-patter of its leafy wings, nor the high-pitched chirrup it issued as it entered her sleep lodge, but the violent jab of its stick finger deep inside her ear.

She erupted from beneath the furs with a howl of pain, swatting at the detestable thing. It made a brief attempt to avoid her wild swings, skirling crazily, before finally seeming to give up and allow her to snatch it out of the air, its purpose now concluded.

Her ear still hot with pain, Nok sat, heart pounding, until the homunculus had finally stopped thudding around inside the loose cage of her fist. Then, blinking gummy sleep from her eyes, she slowly unfurled her fingers to peer at the strange construct.

It had no features to speak of; no eyes, mouth, or anything resembling a head. Just a twist of thin, long-dead branches, bound with desiccated leaves and imbued with anima enough to carry out its single purpose. It squirmed in her palm, as if making ready to jab her again. With a sigh, she closed her fist tight and crushed it.

So. I've been summoned.

Nok rolled her neck, working out the kinks, and then—tossing the crumpled remains of the homunculus to the ground—she dragged herself from the pit of her bed.

The scent of roasting meat from outside the lodge made her stomach growl as she pulled on her breeches and shirt. She slid her knife into the side of her boot, then mussed her hair in an effort to vanquish the last vestiges of sleep. It was getting long; she'd have to crop it again before the week was out. Satisfied, she ducked out of the lodge into the chill morning beyond.

It was well past dawn; the pale sun was high overhead, and the village was crawling with people. She'd overslept. Mother Falamine would be furious. Today, though, she'd have to wait—Nok had more important things to do than fletching arrows and skinning deer.

Close by, Aedle sat outside the neighbouring lodge, hunched over his cooking pot, peering myopically at its pungent contents as he turned his ladle in slow, concentric circles. Beside the pot the plucked carcass of a bird was turning golden brown on an iron spit over the fire. Nok approached.

"Morning, Aedle."

The old man looked up at her, squinting through bushy eyebrows. After a moment he seemed to recognise her, as his shoulders suddenly dropped in resignation and he returned to stirring his pot. "You again." He let out a long, wheezing sigh.

"Don't be like that. I know you take it as a compliment."

"A compliment, is it?" He shook his head. "More like bloody theft!" Nok grinned. They went through this same ritual every day. "Well, get it over with, then. Leave a poor old man to starve."

Nok laughed. Aedle was the most well-fed man in the village. He'd never missed a meal in his life, and had the pick of the hunters' offerings, too; payment, it was said, for a long-ago service to the village. Nok had heard tell that, as a younger man, he had ventured out into the swamplands to fell a beast that was stalking the tribe's younglings. He'd disappeared for nine days and everyone had assumed he'd been taken by the Kith or mauled by the beast, but on the tenth day he had returned with the creature's head and had never once uttered a word about what had occurred. Looking at him now, with his worn, saggy skin and his pot-shaped belly, Nok found it hard to believe that he had ever wielded a blade in anger.

Nevertheless, she knew he secretly enjoyed their morning exchanges, and that he'd cooked the bird for her benefit, despite his grumbling; she could smell the venison broiling in his stew.

"I don't know what I'd do without you, Aedle," she said as she plucked the hot, greasy carcass from the spit. She took a grateful bite, juices running down her chin.

"Wol forbid," he replied. "Now go on, be off with you. Leave an old man to his peace."

Laughing, Nok carried on down the path, munching on the roasted bird as she walked.

The village rarely changed, she considered, as she weaved between trundling carts and boys laden with bundles of hay, drawing disapproving glares from the Mothers. In fact, so far as she could tell, it hadn't changed since the time of Wol himself. Every which way she looked people went about their assigned duties, brewing beer, forging weapons, mending clothes, sowing seeds. She wondered if it would be this way forever.

She'd heard talk of the troubles beyond the swamps, of course—of the mounting armies in the East, the Velinites making ready for war. So, too, had she been ingrained with gruesome tales of the Kith, of their wicked god-who-lived-amongst-them, of what they did to any Wolkin who dared venture west beyond the village boundary.

Her brother, Frik, had once claimed to have seen one of the antler-clad demons skulking in the mist by the low field, but Nok had always known when he was fibbing, embellishing his stories to frighten her. It had worked, too—despite herself, Nok hadn't ventured down to the low field since. Nor had Frik, of course, but that was another story.

"There you are!"

Nok turned at the sound of the familiar, scolding voice, ducking just in time to avoid the swipe of a hand that was intended to strike her upside the head. She lunged out of arm's reach, coming about to see the red-faced Mother Falamine, resplendent in her stark blue robes, glowering at her with untamed fury.

"Where have you been? And what are you doing with *that*?" The woman jabbed a finger at the half-eaten carcass in Nok's hand.

"Breakfast," said Nok, around a mouthful of greasy meat.

The woman's jaw worked for a moment, as if she were about to launch into another tirade, and then she seemed to think better of it. She took a deep breath. Some of the red went out of her rosy cheeks. "It's well past time you were at the skinning house. There's work to be done."

Nok shrugged. "I'm sorry, Mother. I can't today."

The woman flushed again. "What do you mean, you *can't*?"

"I'm needed in the Greenwood. Trith-tree sent a homunculus."

"And where *is* this homunculus?" demanded Mother Falamine, clearly dubious.

"On the floor of my sleep lodge," said Nok. She took another bite from the carcass, wiping her mouth on her sleeve. "The bastard thing stabbed me in the ear."

Mother Falamine seemed to consider this for a moment. "The *ear*?"

Nok nodded. She tossed the remains of the bird into the grass by the side of the path. Two mangy-looking dogs appeared from behind the nearby lodges and began to circle it warily.

Mother Falamine sighed. "Very well. Send my blessings to Trith-tree. And if I find you've been lying to me, girl…"

Nok feigned horror. "As if I would!"

Mother Falamine raised her arm again, preparing for another swing. "Go!"

"I'm going! I'm going!"

The Greenwood marked the northernmost boundary of the Wolkin's territory—a densely packed knot of oaks that stretched, uninterrupted, for twenty or more leagues. Living in such close proximity, the trees and the tribe had forged an almost symbiotic relationship—for centuries the Greenwood's outermost fringes had provided the Wolkin with a sustainable supply of wood, and in turn, the Wolkin offered a steady stream of tributes to the Great Oaks at the heart of the forest.

Nok had never liked the place. There were things in there that stirred at night—shrill cries that rang out from deep amongst the moss-stained boughs and sodden air, voices that seemed to originate in Nok's nightmares. Voices of the long dead returned to haunt her. Worse, perhaps—such sounds reminded her of the one voice she longed to hear, but never would again.

She hugged herself as she trod the narrow path through the trees, her boots leaving shallow impressions in the mossy loam. The air was thick and damp, making her skin feel slick and cold. Dew pattered down from the overhead leaves, drumming on her head and shoulders.

The deeper she delved, the more her hackles prickled. She felt eyes upon her from all directions. While she understood that she was perfectly safe—the trees would make sure of that—intuitively she fought the urge to turn and flee. Nothing about the Greenwood *felt* safe.

Ahead of her, she could hear them whispering to one another, an inhuman soughing that was all the more eerie because of the organs employed to make it. Mouths that were never meant to form such sounds, throats that had been twisted and contorted into new shapes.

Nok swallowed and pressed ahead, bunching her fists by her sides, so hard that her nails dug into the calloused flesh of her palms.

What did Trith-tree want? Why summon her now?

Here, the sunlight barely breached the canopy, falling in thin shafts that seemed to pick out the snaking roots, the dark hollows, the warrens underfoot. It dappled Nok's face and arms, but what should have felt warming, reassuring, only reminded her how far from the village she had come. Out here she was alone, and she might as well have been on a different island.

She glimpsed movement and hesitated, fingers brushing the top of her boot, reaching for her knife—only to realise it was nothing but a branch, sagging in the gentle breeze. She fought for calm, breathing deep, steadying her overwrought heart.

Nearly there now. Soon it'll be over.

It was the stench that hit her first—the sweet, sickly aroma of rotting meat. She gagged, keeping her lips pressed tight together, repressing the urge to eject her breakfast. She wished she'd thought twice about eating the damn bird.

Now the figures were emerging from the gloom as she walked on—human forms, bound to the gnarled boles of the Great Oaks, shifting and trembling erratically, as if some ancient god were attempting to animate them in an approximation of human movement, but failing in every meaningful way to get the details right.

Nok tried not to look at them as she walked amongst them; the remnants of Wolkin dead, bound to the trees in tribute, given over to the tree spirits to merge with them in a strange semblance of the afterlife.

This was the Wolkin's graveyard, the place where she would eventually end her days. The thought appalled her. To have the tree's roots burrow deep into her inanimate flesh, extending its web through her muscles, her nerves, violating her skull to infest her brain. Filling her veins with sap. To resurrect her as something else; a gestalt, a parasite, living on through the tree, sharing her memories with those of the ancient oak. To become the puppet of something else, something *divine*.

She knew it was a great honour. For generations, the Wolkin had submitted themselves in this manner, and the trees had blessed them. The people of her tribe could live on, in a way, and their loved ones might visit them here, in the Greenwood, and so never truly feel their loss.

All except Frik, of course.

She kept her head down as she walked, hurrying her step. Outstretched fingers brushed her arms, and the mumbling, moaning of the dead—again, that terrible whispering—was all she could hear, swirling around her in a rising cacophony. Homunculi flitted to-and-fro, a cloud of spiteful messengers and wardens, darting between trees, whispering in ears that were now as much wood as flesh.

To her left, a figure that had seemingly petrified since her previous visit some weeks ago—the tree had now replaced so much of the original person's flesh that their form was frozen rigid, locked forever in place, a wooden statue where once there had been a man. This was Sarek-tree, one of the oldest of the Wolkin, from the time of Wol himself. His eyes seemed to follow her as she hurried past, and she did not know whether to pity or revere him.

And then she was there, standing before Trith-tree in the grove, and all at once, everything seemed all right.

"Mother."

The figure that wore her mother's face appeared to be asleep, head lolled to one side, arms hanging loosely by her sides. At the sound of Nok's voice she stirred, turning to face the girl, her lips curling slowly into a smile. Moss had crept up one side of her face, and her left shoulder and upper chest had almost entirely been replaced by new, supple shoots, tightly weaved to resemble working muscle.

"You're late, child." Her voice was like the creaking of ancient wood.

"Late is an interesting concept for an entity as old as you," said Nok, with a grin.

"It is not so long since I sat you upon my knee," said Trith-tree. "And yet you are correct. My life amongst the Wolkin now seems so...fleeting. The seasons shall soon change once again. There is a chill in the air."

Nok shrugged. "We'll be ready. We always are."

Trith-tree laughed, but it sounded more like the rustle of branches in the wind than her memory of her mother's gentle chuckle. "Yes. The children of Wol are nothing if not resilient."

Nok kicked absently at the dirt. "Why did you summon me here, Mother?"

"Can a mother not wish to look upon a daughter out of love?"

"*Mother...*"

Trith-tree sighed. She folded her arms across her chest, then unfolded them again almost immediately.

"Spit it out."

"Word amongst the Oak-kin is that Amaranth has been reborn."

Nok frowned. "The Queen of the Broken?"

Trith-tree nodded. "It is her time. The great wheel has turned, and so is she renewed."

Nok was pacing now, back and forth across the grove. Falak-tree and Orlath-tree, her mother's neighbours, were staring at her openly, slack-jawed and wide-eyed. She'd barely noticed them when she'd arrived, her attention focused upon her mother. Falak-tree had always disturbed her—something about his missing right arm and the twist of roots that now erupted from the wrenched socket had always put her on edge. The appendages writhed as he watched her, like the tentacles of one of the swamp-spawned, and she turned away, desperately trying to hide her disgust. She wished they'd leave her in peace, but that wasn't how it worked. There were no secrets here in the Greenwood. No privacy from the Oak-kin.

"What of it? Why should I care if a half-forgotten goddess is reborn in a distant land?" she said.

Trith-tree reached out a hand and beckoned Nok closer with a curled finger. Dutifully, Nok approached. "Listen to me, child. Amaranth belongs to a time before even the Great Oaks raised their mighty boughs from the earth. Her powers are manifold. She might deign to assist us. She is, after all, the patron of broken things."

Nok stared at her mother with sudden understanding. "Frik?"

Trith-tree nodded. "Is there a more broken thing among us than that poor child, for whom the cultivation could never work?"

Nok was breathless. "You...you think Amaranth might *fix* him?"

"I think she is our only hope."

"Then how...?"

For a moment, all in the grove was silent, save for the distant moaning of the unquiet dead.

"You, Nok. You shall take his bones across the swamplands to Amaranth, and you shall beg of her a favour."

"Me?" Nok shook her head. "How can *I* cross the swamplands? I barely know how to wield a skinning knife, let alone a sword!"

"Then a skinning knife shall be your weapon, child." Trith-tree brushed a hand against Nok's cheek. It felt cold, strange, otherworldly. "This you must do. Otherwise Frik will be lost to us forever."

Tears burned in Nok's eyes. This was too much. How could her mother put such a burden upon her shoulders? Was this even her mother speaking, or the *thing* that had infested her corpse? She chewed her lip; tasted blood. "I don't…I mean, I can't…"

But Trith-tree had closed her eyes, and the rustle of the leaves and the creaking of branches had suddenly grown so loud that Nok couldn't think, couldn't make any sense of what was happening. She watched, dumbfounded, as the trunk of the oak began to part, flowering open like a suppurating wound, a sickly bundle pushed forth from inside of it; the macabre progeny of the dead.

Nok grimaced at the sweet stench, the grotesque howling of the surrounding Oak-kin as they raised their voices in lamentation, the slick torrent of sap that oozed from the cavity like arterial blood.

And then, a low moan bubbling from her lips, she dropped to her knees at the sight of the yellowed bones that spilled upon on the mossy ground before her, and wept.

Chapter Two

'To look upon the light of other realms is to ignite a fire in one's soul so pernicious that the mortal world will forevermore be dulled.'
                    Brother Rodoric, Book of Remonstrance

THE BELLS WERE TOLLING FOR EVENING PRAYER, but all Ambrose could think about was his bed: a soft, downy divan, draped in glorious silken sheets, with goose feather pillows scented with lavender and bergamot. It called to him from across the chamber like a serenading siren, threatening to beach him upon its shore. And beach him it would, for he was a man of ample proportions, who had dedicated his bountiful years to the many finer things in life.

Evening prayer, to such a man, was just one of life's many burdens to be overcome.

Indeed, the Pantheon had never deigned to grant his prayers—at least not directly—but he begged they might grant him this, a night of joyous reprieve. Would it really make that much of a difference if, just this once, his lone voice was absent from the choir?

Alas, it was not to be, for no sooner had he convinced himself that his brothers would nary notice him missing, than he heard the familiar hiss of the Prefect's voice in the passageway outside his door, spitting asinine commands to those of the Lower Order foolish enough to get in his way.

The Prefect was, without doubt, a most odious individual, who had not been blessed with either intelligence or dignity, nor—in Ambrose's studied opinion—a particularly handsome aspect. Thus, such a man had had little recourse but the monastery, for few have time and patience for an ugly man with no manners. Not that Ambrose was at all given to such shallow considerations. He was, after all, Arch-Brother-Imperialis of the Upper Order of the Unanswered, and well beyond such base thoughts.

With a sigh, he abandoned his platter of sweets, dusting his sugary fingers and dipping them in the perfumed water bowl by the door. He flicked the ensuing droplets from his fingertips with a delicate wave of his hand.

There was a rap on the door; the sharp *rat-a-tat* of the Prefect's staff upon the wood. Ambrose paused for a moment, collected himself, and then turned the handle.

"Ah, felicitations of the day to you, honourable Prefect."

The man stared at him for a moment with barely supressed rage. "The bells toll for evening prayer," he said, his voice rising in pitch as he struggled to contain himself.

"They do?" said Ambrose, feigning ignorance. He cocked his head. "Ah, yes. You are correct, dear Prefect. I hear them now."

"Arch-Brother-Imperialis—your rooms are almost directly beneath the bell tower."

Ambrose nodded sagely. "Indeed. I fear that years of aural abuse—perpetrated by said bells—have done for my delicate ears. I am, in fact, at a loss."

"Well consider yourself lost no longer. I shall lead the way." The

Prefect, eyes narrowing suspiciously, stepped to one side and ushered Ambrose into the passageway.

"It is most advantageous you found yourself passing my door at this late hour," said Ambrose, as they fell into step. "Indeed, this is quite the circuitous route from your chamber to the Hall of Windows."

"Mmmm," mumbled the Prefect. "An evening constitutional."

"Then you, too, were running late to evening prayer!" said Ambrose. "Oh dear, we must maintain a dignified front when we arrive. The Prefect is, after all, responsible for setting a good example to the rest of us, is he not?"

"I wasn't running late!" the Prefect spluttered. "I was... I was..."

"Fear not, dear Brother. Your secret shall remain safe with me." Ambrose touched his fingers to his lips in conspiratorial solidarity and tried to hide his smile.

Evening song had already begun as the two men arrived by the entranceway to the Hall of Windows, and Ambrose felt the Prefect hesitate on the threshold, as though unsure what etiquette might dictate in such dire circumstance. Ambrose could see the little wrinkles on the man's forehead forming deep furrows as he frowned, the single bead of sweat trickling down the side of his pugilist's nose.

He stepped forward, taking the other man firmly by the arm. "This way, Prefect. Follow my lead."

The man nodded mutely in response.

Ambrose led them through the doorway into the vast chamber beyond. Here, the gathered Brothers of the Upper Order stood on rows of tiered benches, their serene faces upturned to the view. Light played down upon them in swirling patterns; the majestic glow of other realms, glimpsed through the towering windows that hung from the vaulted ceiling. The wordless song ebbed and flowed as the monks ululated and chanted their praise to the Pantheon.

Ambrose led the Prefect around to the back of the gathered choir, to where a small observation area had been set aside. This, Ambrose had long since claimed as his preferred spot, for it afforded him the luxury of a stunning view without drawing the attention of his Brothers whenever he arrived late. Which, by no fault of his own, happened to occur most evenings.

Beside Ambrose, the Prefect relaxed, stretching his arms as he limbered up to join the song. Ambrose groaned inwardly. Was the man so restlessly pious that he could not forgo his tuneless accompaniment for a single evening?

Pushing the man's insistent wailing from his mind, Ambrose focused upon the windows themselves. This, he had always enjoyed—this moment where he was blessed to look out upon the vistas of the sacred underworlds, to feel the light of their strange suns warming his face—to bask, for a moment, in their otherworldly grandeur. Standing there, he felt himself upon the threshold of a liminal space, almost as if he might raise himself up and step through one of those windows, to stand amongst the soaring peaks of the Daliquish, or walk beneath the rosy skies of the Ullness, or traverse the crooked bone roads of the Hosst.

Such thoughts were food for his very soul, and as such, he gorged himself. One day, he would walk those paths. Yet such a journey was not for him, not yet. Only the dear departed could claim such an honour, and, as Ambrose was fond of reminding the Prefect, there was life in the Arch-Brother-Imperialis yet.

Tired already of the lights and the monotonous singing—for a few minutes under such trying conditions had a tendency to stretch like *years*—Ambrose quietly stepped down from his perch and made for the gloomy passageway at the rear of the chamber. A passageway that the Prefect had so far failed to acquaint himself with, for the building was some centuries old and maintained its secrets well, and the Prefect only thirty-seven and lacking in inquisitiveness as well as beauty. Even now, he remained where Ambrose had placed him, head thrown back in wonderment, chest puffed-out like a peacock in heat, his aquamarine robes tossed open like ruffled feathers. If he'd noticed Ambrose's dextrous escape, he gave no sign of it.

And thus, Ambrose took his leave, thoughts of that downy bed once more circling in his mind.

"Hold there, Ambrose!"

With a heavy sigh, heart sinking like a stone dropped in a still millpond, Ambrose froze in his tracks. He was only a few yards from the door to his chamber. A few yards further from his bed. Why did the gods have to punish him so?

He turned, confident that he had concealed his profound disappointment. "Leofric. What ails you so, that you must lurk in shrouded passageways to set upon unwary travellers as they pass?"

"Pantheon abound, man! You look as though a thousand Hosstians were feasting on your withered soul."

Perhaps, Ambrose reflected, his powers of concealment were not as developed as he had allowed. "Why aren't you at evening prayer?" he muttered, by way of deflection.

"Much too busy for all that," said Leofric, waving a dismissive hand. A fat, glistening leech was perched upon the back of it, engorged with the man's blood. Ambrose wondered if he'd noticed. "Besides, I could ask the same of you."

"You could," said Ambrose, "but surely that would only succeed in delaying you further, and I fear we've already wandered quite some distance from the point at hand."

Leofric glowered. He wrinkled his nose, causing his spectacles to ride up and down its shining slope. "The *point*, Arch-Brother-Imperialis, is that the Chief Prognosticator has sent for you. Apparently, it is a matter of some urgency."

For a moment, Ambrose considered bolting for his chamber.

Perhaps he could barricade the door, hold them off for a few hours of blissful, stolen solitude. But he knew it was only a passing dream. He'd have to emerge for his supper, after all, not to mention his bath, and they'd almost certainly be waiting to pounce. Such was his life; a constant battle in which he was fated to never win. No, whatever it was, he might as well get it over with. "Very well," he said, reluctantly.

Leofric looked momentarily taken aback by this unexpected capitulation. "Are you certain you're quite well, Ambrose?"

"No," muttered Ambrose, striking out down the passageway for the Prognosticarium. "But sometimes one must recognise a higher calling."

Little did he know that they were words that he would soon come to regret.

"Ah, Arch-Brother-Imperialis. I'm so pleased you could be excused from evening prayer."

Ambrose coughed, then dabbed at his forehead with a folded silk kerchief. "Quite so, quite so. I was...um...led to believe the matter warranted a certain degree of urgency." He looked expectantly at the Chief Prognosticator. The man was an oddity, to say the least. Ambrose had never been comfortable in his presence. Something to do with the eyes. And maybe the ears. Or perhaps the claw-like appendage that had once been a hand, but had been burnt to a near crisp during an accident and never properly restored. Or—Ambrose reflected—most likely it was his nasally voice, a sound that seemed to inspire paroxysms of distaste in Ambrose's gullet, each and every time the man spoke.

"Indeed, yes. There has been a *development*." Now the man was attempting to sound profound. The Order really was doomed.

"And what *development* is that?"

"I'll show you," said the Chief Prognosticator, positively glowing. He raised his hand and snapped his fingers, and from the arched recesses that ran around the edges of the chamber there emerged a squall of hooded figures, scurrying hither and thither like stooped-back rats. The Chief Prognosticator grinned triumphantly as, moments later, the figures formed up into an orderly column—two wide and seven long—their sandaled feet arranged upon a clearly delineated grid upon the floor. A hush settled upon them, then, like a sudden inhalation.

Ambrose studied the face of the Chief Prognosticator. The man's smile was rigid. His eyes flicked towards the ceiling. Curious, Ambrose followed the man's gaze.

Something stirred in the rafters. A chain clunked through a pulley, its wheel creaking in complaint. Ambrose squinted. There were men up there, balanced upon the wooden beams, feeding out the heavy chain.

"What in all the under-realms is going on?" said Ambrose, waving a finger at the ceiling. "What are those men *doing* up there?"

The Chief Prognosticator merely touched his finger to his lips in response, before turning back to the events unfurling above.

Stupefied, Ambrose watched as on object finally hove into view, dangling precariously from the end of the chain—an enormous brass key. It was the length of a horse and as thick as a man's thigh, with a finial of exquisitely cast knotwork and—he realised now—served as the companion piece to an equally enormous keyhole in a set of double doors at the far end of the chamber.

And so the ritual unfolded, as the key was slowly lowered onto the waiting shoulders of the fourteen arrayed figures—presumably brothers requisitioned from the Lower Order—who then, in studied silence, marched the key forward to the waiting doors. Without even a groan of protest from amongst them, the men hefted the key—evidently the reason for the pronounced stoops in their gait—and slid it into the keyhole. Then, each of them taking his place upon the shaft, they slowly turned it until the mechanism clinked loudly as the lock was released. The door swung open on creaking hinges.

There was a palpable sense of relief from all in the room.

"Extraordinary," said Ambrose, for he was unsure what other words would suffice to describe the outlandish display. "And beyond that door is your office?"

The Chief Prognosticator sniggered. "My office? Oh, no, Arch-Brother-Imperialis. *That* is the Chamber of Witness."

"Of course," said Ambrose. "Forgive me." He started towards the open door, then paused and glanced back at the Chief Prognosticator. "And what, precisely, are we about to witness?"

The Chief Prognosticator shrugged. "Merely the birth of a god," he said.

"So, Amaranth is reborn," said the Prefect, drumming his fingertips upon the table. "You do understand what this means?"

They were gathered in the Refectory, all the scions of the Upper Order, seated around the large ebony table at the centre of the room. The moonlight was slanting in through the towering windows to fall in shafts upon the polished wood, picking out the bowl of sugared plums that was, alas, just out of Ambrose's reach. Once again, he cursed his luck. He was not having a good day.

"That a new window shall have to be erected in the hall," said Beorth, scratching nervously at the thin patch of hair behind his ear.

"Yes, yes," snapped the Prefect. "Of course. But I'm talking about the opportunity it presents for the Order."

"You seek the patronage of this reborn god?" said Leofric, before taking a long swig from a cup of beer. How had he laid his hands upon that?

The Prefect sighed. "No more than the Order seeks the patronage of all amongst the Pantheon." He pushed his chair back from the table and rose. He began pacing, circling the table and its gathered occupants, hands clasped tightly behind his back. Was he attempting to hide a tremble in said limbs? Had there been a quaver in his voice only moments before?

The man was afflicted, Ambrose realised. Troubled by the words he was preparing to speak. It did not bode well. "No. I speak of something that cuts to the very heart of our Order." He paused dramatically and turned, meeting their eyes, each in turn. "I speak of the *Question*."

"Heresy!" barked the Chief Prognosticator.

"You cannot be serious, Prefect," said Ambrose. "It is a fundamental tenet of our belief that the Question should forever remain unanswered."

The Prefect was still circling like a predatory shark, growing in confidence as he spoke. "So we have long believed. So countless generations have blindly upheld. But I ask you this: what purpose serves a question that is never asked? Should we not strive to uncover the truth? Is it not our *duty*?"

"And you believe Amaranth could provide that answer?" said Aeofon, whom Ambrose had always considered to be a wily toad.

"Indeed, I do," said the Prefect. "For Amaranth is the Queen of the Broken, and is it not her burden but to fix things?"

"This is a dangerous path," said Ambrose. "Even if Amaranth deigned to grant us audience, what if we do not like the answer we are given? What then for our Order? Is it not better to ponder blindly than to wallow in surety? For surely, the answer could never provide more succour than the scholarly imaginings of those who anticipate its asking?"

"Think, though, of the rewards such certainty might offer. Think of the followers who might flock to our cause, of the ascent of our Order, the strengthening of our faith. Think of that," said the Prefect.

"It is a grave risk," said Leofric. "You would gamble all for a single roll of the dice."

"Ah," said the Prefect, wagging his finger as he circled back around to his chair, "but therein lies the beauty of my plan. It takes but one pair of lips to utter a question, and one pair of ears to hear its reply." He reached forward and snatched a sugared plum from the bowl, tearing at it obscenely with his teeth. Ambrose's mouth watered at the sight.

"Then you propose we send an emissary," said Aeofon, "to bear the Question to her?"

"Quite so," said the Prefect, flecks of juicy plum flesh spattering the table. "And one to bear the burden of her answer. He, and he alone, shall be charged with deciding whether to share it."

"A…satisfactory solution," said the Chief Prognosticator. "Although it becomes clear that this individual must be one whom is held in the highest regard of the Order. One whose judgement and insight is beyond reproach."

"Then we are decided?" said the Prefect.

Leofric nodded. "Aye."

Ambrose glanced at the shining faces, as, in turn, each of them nodded their assent.

"Ambrose?"

Startled, he turned to the Prefect. "What?"

The Prefect sounded exasperated. "Are you in agreement?"

Slowly, Ambrose nodded. There seemed little point in battling consensus. Perhaps, after this, he might finally make it to his bed. "Yes, yes. Agreed."

"Excellent." The Prefect clapped his hands.

"Now, as to the matter of whom shall undertake this honoured task…?" ventured Aeofon. Ambrose almost laughed out loud. What a fool, angling for such a hideous undertaking. A dangerous water crossing, a carriage ride through untamed wildling territory and a petition to an uncaring god. And no doubt the undying gratitude of all his brothers in the Order—provided he did not design to protect them from the truth or go insane in its hearing. No, Ambrose would merrily support Aeofon's application for such a role.

"Ah, that is a matter that is already settled," said the Prefect. "It has ever been the role of the Arch-Brother-Imperialis to act as emissary on behalf of the Order."

Ambrose erupted into a startled cough. Was that his heart, attempting to burst clear of his chest? "What? No, no. I couldn't possibly. You heard the Chief Prognosticator. This requires a better man than I."

"Nonsense," said the Prefect. "You're exactly the man for the job. I won't hold with modesty, Arch-Brother-Imperialis. We shall hear nothing of your protests. We all have faith in you."

"But I…I…"

'Sometimes one must recognise a higher calling, Ambrose," said Leofric, an amused gleam in his eye.

Inwardly, Ambrose groaned. He reached for a sugared plum. It might well be the last he would taste in a while.

Chapter Three

Across blasted heath
And rolling moors
'twixt raging peaks
And ever more—
He walks

This lowly knight
He seeks no crown
No storied riches
Not hope, renown—
He walks

Towards life or death
It matters not
For each and both
Shall be his lot –
He walks

He walks

He walks

    The Ballad of Perisher Oswald, Traditional

PALLOR OPENED HIS EYES, WINCED, AND THEN rolled onto his side to avoid the lancing spears of sunlight intent upon searing his mind. The room took a moment to catch up. His stomach balked, threatening to void itself. He fought down the urge, sucking at the air through dry, cracked lips. His tongue felt like a rattan matt.

"It's time to get up, milord."

Pallor groaned at the sound of the woman's voice. What was Stonn doing here, in his room? In fact, come to think of it, where exactly *was* here? He didn't even remember taking a room.

"Here. Some water."

Stonn pushed the flagon towards his face. Pallor winced again.

"Yes, all right, Stonn. Give me a moment."

"It's almost noon," said Stonn, and Pallor couldn't help but pick up on the insinuating tone. *You should have been up hours ago.*

"What of it?" He stifled another groan as he pushed himself up onto his elbow. The room swam. He tried to focus on Stonn, who was kneeling beside the bed, eyes narrowed in disapproval.

"You don't remember, do you?"

"Remember *what*?" He snatched the proffered flagon from Stonn's grasp and gulped down the tepid liquid. It eased his dry throat and lips but felt as if it were curdling whatever was in his stomach.

"What the prophet told you last night in the bar."

"That sounds like the beginning of a bad joke, Stonn."

The squire sighed and got to her feet. "It's probably for the best," she said, picking up his discarded clothes.

Pallor slumped back into the soft caress of the pillow. *The prophet.* Now she came to mention it, there was a half-remembered thought, lingering in the back of his mind.

He closed his eyes, tried to concentrate.

A woman. Dark-skinned, beautiful. A tattooed throat, like a spider-web. Riding him like a bucking horse in this very bed.

No. That came later.

A filthy gutter snipe who stank of piss. One blind eye, milky and glazed. One sharp as a thief's dagger. A gap-toothed smile. Coins crossing palms.

"This prophet. He looked like a shit-smeared child?" He peered at Stonn, who was by the foot of the bed, now, stuffing Pallor's clothes into the travelling case.

"No. That was the homeless boy you paid to fetch her from the temple."

"So she *was* the dark-skinned woman with the tattoo."

"Wrong again, milord. That was the woman who emptied your purse and fled after you passed out mid-way through—"

"All right, all right. So that wasn't her." He rubbed a hand over his chin. It was rough with half a day's worth of bristles. "Hold on—she *robbed* me?" He sat up, immediately wishing he hadn't.

Stonn shrugged. "Well, you were rather indiscreet with your coin, if I recall. Everyone in the inn knew you'd just been paid for the draugr job."

Pallor tried to circle back through the jumbled events that were now crowding his memory. He had a sudden, sharp recollection of buying everyone a drink. The whole bar. Waving his coin around like it was going out of fashion. He winced. He'd basically invited them to rob him. But that was *after* the prophet, wasn't it?

"This prophet—what did they say?"

Stonn closed the travelling case and turned to look at him. She was holding a clean set of breeches and a folded shirt. She tossed them on the bed. "Are you sure you want to know?"

"Well of course I want to know. I wouldn't have asked, otherwise."

"She told you—in her typically cryptic and portentous way—about a keep a few leagues from here, where a goddess has recently been reborn."

Pallor had a sudden vision of a bald-headed woman with scarified patterns upon her cheeks and a smear of green dye across her eyelids and the bridge of her nose. The woman was leaning forward, breathing heavily through rotted teeth. She was repeating a name, slowly and loudly: *Amaranth*. Pallor shivered.

"A worthy foe for a Knight of Perish."

Stonn nodded. "That's what you said last night. Right before you declared to the whole inn that you were setting out this morning to challenge her to mortal combat."

Pallor remembered cheering. And more drinks. That was when he'd met the woman who'd robbed him. "Well, perhaps I was a trifle optimistic, eh?" He threw the sheets aside and swung his legs out of the bed. Across the room, Stonn visibly winced. "What—oh." He grabbed the breeches and tugged them on while Stonn turned her back. "She didn't steal my underwear too, did she?"

"What? No, of course not. Why would she?"

"Well, some people like that kind of thing. Perhaps she wanted a trophy, a reminder of her conquest."

"More likely she wanted to get out of here as quickly as possible."

"Hmmph." Pallor stood, tugging on his shirt. "It's all right, you can turn around now. Your dignity is preserved."

"It's not *my* dignity I'm worried about," said Stonn.

Pallor studied her for a moment. Something was different. The usual formless leather breeches and baggy shirt, the scuffed boots and cracked leather belt scabbard. The boyish face with the heavy brows. The disapproving eyes. "Ah! You've cut your hair."

"And?"

"Well, it's...short."

"Truly, you are a master of perception, milord."

Pallor kneaded the muscles around his neck and shoulders. "It's early, Stonn. Perhaps you could be a little more forgiving."

"It's past midday," said Stonn. "And I'm not the forgiving sort."

Pallor was tucking his shirt into his breeches. He stopped. "She didn't take my weapons, did she? Or my armour?"

"Just your coin," said Stonn. "Which is plenty enough. You'd promised me a bonus."

"And I'll honour it," said Pallor, scowling as he resumed tucking his shirt into his decidedly tight waistband. "Just as soon as I can replenish what's been lost."

"It wasn't *lost*," countered Stonn.

"No. Perhaps not. But I shall try to think kindly of the poor young lady who was forced to lay siege to my heart in order to get by."

Stonn snorted. "She's no longer poor, and she was very definitely no *lady*."

Pallor studiously ignored the comment. "Come on. It's time for breakfast. I cannot set about my knightly duty without a hearty meal."

"You intend to go through with it, then?"

"Breakfast? Why yes, of course."

"The goddess," said Stonn, shaking her head in exasperation. "You're going to challenge her?"

"Of course, dear Stonn. In pursuit of a magnificent death, I know no bounds. My journey through the underworlds awaits!"

Stonn beckoned him towards the door. "Yes, milord. After breakfast though, eh?"

"Who's this then?"

The landlady peered across the bar at Stonn, lips pursed. "She's not a regular. And she ain't paid for no room."

Pallor smiled his most gracious smile and swept into a low bow. The gesture made him feel a little unwell. "Good morrow, dear lady. Need I remind you that I am Pallor, Knight of Perish, and this is my boy, Stonn."

"Boy? That's not a—"

"I am the equal of *any* boy…" warned Stonn, a hard note in her voice. Her chin jutted alarmingly, and Pallor worried for a moment that she might gut the presumptuous landlady then and there.

The woman made a harrumphing sound and folded her arms across her chest. "Well, what do you want?"

"Some breakfast," said Pallor. The woman pulled a face. "This *is* an inn, is it not?"

"Yes. But it's gone midday and you haven't yet settled your bill from last night. You were rather generous, if I recall. We had to crack a second barrel." She drummed her fingertips on the bar.

Pallor reached for his purse. And then remembered it was no longer there. He coughed into his fist. "Stonn, pay the lady."

Stonn glowered at him. She unhitched her own purse from her belt and emptied the contents onto the bar, spilling silver and gold coins over the woman's shoes in a sudden, noisy cascade.

"Oi!"

Stonn pushed the now-empty purse into Pallor's hands. "That's the last of it," she said, turning towards the door.

"Hold on, what about breakfast?"

"Looks like we're chasing rabbits again, doesn't it?" She stopped in the doorway, glancing back to make sure he was following. "I hope it was worth it."

Pallor shrugged. He was about to tell her it most definitely was—at least what he could remember of it—but then decided against it. He followed her out into the sunshine.

Here on the edge of the village the ground was covered in a thick layer of frost, the distant treetops still clinging resolutely to the last of the previous day's snow. Despite the glaring sun, the air was sharp as cut silk, and his breath fogged. At least, he considered, it might help to clear his head.

Around the inn, people bustled with their daily industry. "Here, you, man," Pallor called out to a stable hand, who was brushing down the sweat-lathered flanks of a fine gelding whose owner had evidently just arrived.

"Yes, sir?"

"Bring my horse around, if you would? I've a mind to be on my way."

The man looked at him, red-faced and lost for words. "Umm…"

"Well?"

Beside Pallor, Stonn sighed. Again. She seemed to be doing a lot of that this morning.

"The thing is, sir…" the man stammered, clearly embarrassed. "The fact of the matter is…"

"She took your horse," said Stonn, cutting him off. The stable hand gave an embarrassed nod. He looked relieved.

"Of course she did," said Pallor, his voice dripping with resignation. "The harridan obviously needed a quick getaway."

Stonn smirked. "You've changed your tune."

"To pilfer a man's coin is one thing, Stonn. To force him to walk is quite another." He turned back towards the door. "Come. I believe we have some repacking ahead of us."

The campfire crackled and spat, ashen fireflies drifting languorously on the chill currents. Here, amongst the towering red-barked conifer trees, they seemed shut off from the outside world, a tiny island in a frigid ocean of frost and snow. The inn and the village were lost to the gloaming, several miles distant, and Pallor's earlier, salutary mood had given way to a maudlin sense of regret.

He took another bite of the stringy, greasy meat. He chewed it quickly and swallowed it down with a gulp. It was a far cry from the roasted boar he'd filled his belly with the previous night, or the feast he'd anticipated for breakfast that morning.

Stonn had caught the mangy hare as they'd trod through the hard-packed snow in the shadow of the great trees. She'd been silent, reproachful, as she'd trudged, and Pallor had been left to his thoughts.

And such thoughts they were—of the woman who had stolen not only his purse and his horse, but quite possibly his heart...along with what was left of his dignity. *Imalia*. That had been her name. Or at least the name she'd given. And she had been spectacular. Not just in the way she had ridden him—although his returning memory of that had brought quite a smile to his parched lips—but in the way she had woven her spell, in the confident way she had carried herself, in the wit she had demonstrated as she'd undermined each of his well-worn tales of glory and danger.

"You're thinking about that woman again, aren't you?"

Pallor frowned. "How can you tell?"

"The wistful expression, the sad, lonely eyes—the fact you suddenly stopped chewing with a mouth full of meat..."

"Oh, do be quiet, Stonn."

The woman sniggered. She was warming her hands over the fire. "She was quite something to behold, I'll give you that."

"Aye. She was," agreed Pallor. He tossed the remains of the hare into the fire, raising a shower of sparks. "She was that."

They sat in silence for the moment, the only sounds the whispering of the breeze through the treetops high above, and the distant chatter of a night-chough.

Pallor leaned back against the bole of a tree and looked at Stonn. Her face was under-lit by the glow of the fire, lean and hard-lined, but handsome all the same. Why did she still follow him? It wasn't for the coin, that much was certain. The adventure? Perhaps. But then she always seemed to face it with such reluctance, despite her deftness in battle. And she showed little interest in swelling the ranks of the Knights of Perish.

He knew she wanted to prove herself, to show the world she was as proud and strong and deserving as any man. But she had already done so, many times over. He found it difficult to fathom why she remained at his side. What would she do when he passed from this world to the next, to make his long journey through the underworld? Would she await his return?

He realised she was looking straight at him. "Are you sure you want to do this?" she said after a moment, her voice level.

"Do what?"

"Don't play games. You *know* what. Take on a god. It cannot end well."

Pallor laughed, but it lacked his usual bombastic mirth. "That, dear Stonn, is precisely the point."

She'd taken up a stick and was prodding at the embers of the fire, staring deep into the dancing flames. "This is madness, Pallor. You have nothing to prove. To anyone. Least of all an outdated knightly order on an island half a world away. So what if you do this? So what if the Broken Queen tears you asunder and casts your spirit into the underworld? So what if you face your so-called trials and manage to find your way back to this realm?" She flung the stick into the flames. "What purpose will it have served? All you'll have done is walked in a circle."

"Perhaps walking in a circle is better than standing still," he said, quietly. "Perhaps it's not about proving myself to anyone but me. I've walked this path my entire life. Would you really have me abandon it now?"

"Just because you've walked a way along the wrong road does not mean you must accept the wrong destination," said Stonn.

"Perhaps for some," agreed Pallor, "but for others, they're too far gone to even consider turning about."

Stonn gave a curt nod and stood, crossing to her bedroll.

For a while, Pallor remained staring into the flames, before he, too, lay down for a while to rest. In the distance, some shrill beast screeched into the night, startling the birds, and sending a chill finger running along Pallor's spine.

Chapter Four

'And so did Amaranth rise again to claim her broken throne, and the carrion birds did sing, for their mother was renewed.'

SATER JON, ON THE CURSE OF EVER-LIVING

HIS LEGS WERE CREAKING AGAIN. HE'D HAVE TO see to that. A touch of millengrass oil and some pig grease should ease up the fractious joints. For a while, at least. It wouldn't be long before they'd need replacing altogether, and that would be an entirely more cumbersome undertaking. He didn't relish the idea.

Not for the first time that day, Sleath cursed. His had been a long life, far longer than most, and longer still than he should have wanted. A life filled with endless years of anticipation—in effect, a form of near-hibernation—punctuated by brief spans of fevered activity in the company of his mistress. How long had it been since her last manifestation? Seven, eight hundred years? And for what? A mere handful of decades, before she withered again and died, returning to wherever it was she went between times. Slipping through the cracks in what passed in this world for reality.

He supposed he should have felt excitement at the presence of this newly birthed avatar, but in truth, he had grown too old, too weary, and saw only the inevitability of her passing and the long hiatus that would once again ensue. A long life had given him a long view, so that even the lifespans of gods seemed like butterflies.

He sighed. Since when had he become so cynical? The servants of gods were supposed to be devout, were they not? To bask in the glow of their patrons, to revel in their divinity. All he wanted was to get it over with. To go back to tottering around in this tumbledown keep, careless— save for the maintenance of his strange and uncomfortable body.

He supposed he should focus on the matter at hand. It had taken him half a day of poking around in the musty cellars to search out the spyglass Amaranth had requested: a battered cylinder of gold and brass with a fractured lens. The hairline cracks formed a spiderweb through the glass which, when he'd lifted it to his eye, obscured much of the view. But seeing wasn't entirely the point, he knew. At least, not in *that* way.

At the end of the passageway, the door to the tower stood closed. He approached, pulling his robes tighter around his stooped frame to stave off the chill. He raised his fist to knock—

"Come in, Sleath. Do not stand on ceremony."

Shrugging, he lifted the iron latch and eased the door open on its thick, iron hinges. "When you're as old as we are, mistress, ceremony is all we have."

Amaranth laughed. "Yes, I suppose you're right."

She was standing with her back to him, gazing out of the tall window at the frigid scene below. Great gusts stirred drifts of fallen snow, raising them up like swirling devils, cackling gleefully as they played and caroused across the landscape. Here, there were no cottages, no inns. Here, there was nothing but the wilderness and the trees and the elements, warring amongst themselves, encircling the keep as if intent on laying siege to it. And yet they never did, for even the roots and vines and creeping things of the land seemed to hold this place in high esteem, hungry, but never truly encroaching, shy of claiming the half-ruined building as their own.

All except the snow, that was. Where the roof of the tower had crumbled, tumbling flakes had been admitted, falling softly to form a pure, white drift against the wall. Even now they swirled, like flakes of ash, the remnants of a life reduced to cinders.

Amaranth was dressed in white, just like the snow, her airy gown almost translucent in the soft light. Centuries ago he might have felt a stirring at such a sight, but now such thoughts led to nothing but regret.

"I heard you coming," she said, turning to regard him with her strange, fractured eyes. They resembled nothing so much as the broken lens of the spyglass he had brought—which he now set upon the table—and not for the first time he wondered what the world must look like through such eyes; always shattered and imperfect, like something fragile and flawed.

"My legs," he said, by way of explanation. "I shall see to them presently."

"Faithful to the last, dearest Sleath. It has been some time. I shall see to it that you are properly repaired."

Again.

"Forgive me, mistress, but might it not be time to consider a renewal, a revitalisation? Surely it is not beyond your power, and I would serve you all the better if I were young and able-bodied once again." This was a conversation they had had countless times before; an age-old argument in which both were content to play out their eternal roles.

Amaranth approached, laying her hands upon his shoulders. She smelled of the air just after a storm; fresh but charged with something uncanny. "Something broken and repaired is something cared for. Something cherished and precious. You, my love, could never be replaced."

Yet my limbs and organs, my flesh and bone—they are all fair game?

But the harsh words would not form on his lips. Perhaps the goddess still held some power over him, after all.

He nodded, and she smiled, turning back to the window. Now, there was a glass of wine in her hand that had not been there a moment before. She sipped from it thoughtfully. "I had forgotten what it was like to taste wine," she said, "to enjoy the simple pleasures of the physical realm." She stood in silence for a moment. "When I die—it is a real death, of sorts. A passing from one state to another. Every time, I remember that loss. I mourn it."

"I'm sorry," said Sleath. There seemed to be nothing else *to* say.

"We are all of us broken in our way," she said, placing the wine glass on the windowsill and turning to collect the spyglass from where he had placed it. "Do you think they will come?" She looked at him suddenly, and there was something in her eyes he had never seen before—*need*. This was new. This was *interesting*.

"Who, mistress?"

"My pilgrims, of course?"

"Aye. Even now, word of your return spreads amongst the soothsayers and the prophets, the foolish and the wise. Birds chatter. Sleepers dream. The faithful have set out upon their crooked paths, even if they do not yet know it. Yes, they will come, by boat and by road and by mountain pass. Soon they shall wait by your door."

Amaranth nodded. "Ever the comfort, Sleath. Then I shall study the fractures and seek them out." She raised the spyglass to her eye and turned back to the window. Whatever she was seeing, it was no longer the fields of ice and snow, the wheeling birds, the dusted treetops.

For a while, Sleath remained where he stood; silent, patient. Then, when it became clear that his presence was no longer wanted nor required, he turned from the chamber and left, his creaking limbs echoing down the passageway as he walked.

Chapter Five

The spirits of the Greenwood,
To answer such bleak transgression,
Did deign to mould a champion,
A babe in arms,
To grow fierce and learn the many ways of death.
So, swaddled was he,
In vine and branch,
And instilled with dreams of vengeance.
    THE QUIETUS CODEX, ATTRIBUTION UNKNOWN

THE SWAMP STANK.

Worse than the Greenwood with its thick aroma of rotting corpses. Worse than the festering cesspit at the back of old Aedle's lodge. Worse, even, than the ripe, pustulant belly wound that had finally seen her shit of a father off to the netherwoods.

"I can see why our people choose to avoid this place, Frik," she said, as she dragged the paddle through the gloopy water, shaking off a clump of stringy vines that had attached themselves to the shaft. The water oozed around the dugout, grey and opaque, harbouring Who-knew-what beneath its tepid surface.

The air here was chill and wreathed in milky fog. It seemed to linger in her lungs, thick and cloying, as if it were something insidious, trying to infect her like it had infected everything else in this miserable, gloomy place. It clung to the trees that lined the banks, swirled over the surface of the water, seeped through her clothes to leave her skin feeling damp and cold. There was no reprieve. Nothing to break the eerie monotony.

Nothing, that was, save a scattering of tiny lights, hovering in the distance like pinpricks through the murk, yellow orbs adrift in the grey.

"What do you suppose they are, Frik? Way markers?" She angled the dugout towards the nearest of them and pushed the boat along, the water sloshing as she stirred the otherwise-still water.

Frik was by her feet, safe in the burlap sack she had taken from the village stores. He'd proven surprisingly heavy, carting him over her shoulder—along with her bag of provisions—as she'd ventured out beyond the village bounds, down through the low field to the river's edge that marked the boundary of her tribe's territory to the West. There had been no sign of the antler-clad demons here that Frik had once spoken of, but nonetheless, she'd felt a frisson of trepidation as she'd emerged from the long grass onto the riverbank, prepared to run at any moment if one of the dreaded things had risen from the water, feral and keening.

All she had found, though, was a sleeping fisherman, dozing in the sun beneath the shade of a tree. She recognised him as Pendlek, son of Maedle, a spiteful man ten years her senior, who had taken great delight in tormenting Frik during their youthful days. She'd found Pendlek's dugout a little further downstream, dragged up onto the muddy bank, and had felt no compunction in alleviating him of it, pushing it out into the fast-flowing river and hauling Frik hurriedly inside.

That had been three days ago. Since then, she'd followed a tributary deeper into the swamplands, skirting Kith territory and making what progress she could through the foul, treacherous waters. Beyond the swamplands lay a long stretch of forest—or so she understood—which rose steadily towards the frigid wilderness where Amaranth's ruined keep could be found.

Nok's stomach growled. She was tired and hungry. More than once, she had cursed Trith-tree for sending her on this journey. She'd craved adventure, yes—but never had she wanted *this*—to be out here alone in the swamplands, soon to stand face-to-face with a god. If she even survived that long.

She'd been sleeping in the dugout, dragging it up onto firm land and covering herself in the broad, flat leaves of the arbaya plants that grew along the edge of the water here. The nights were the worst; long, lonely and cold, when every sound outside the dugout described some imagined beast, slithering up from the water on its belly to wrestle her out of her hiding hole and rend her with its terrible jaws.

Frik being close was her only comfort, and she wished he could offer her a word of encouragement now, just like he used to. A kind word to appease her dread. That, she reminded herself, was why she was doing this, after all. Why she was out here risking everything. To plead with Amaranth to fix him, so that Nok could take him home again, back to the Greenwood, where he might finally bond with a Great Oak and be reborn, just like Amaranth herself. None in the tribe or amongst the oak-kin understood why the cultivation had failed, what it was about Frik that had rejected the burrowing tendrils of the tree—but perhaps Amaranth might see the truth of it. For Frik was, if nothing else, a broken thing.

Nok fished a strip of dried meat from the pouch inside her coat and chewed on it thoughtfully as she rowed on towards the light. What would Frik make of all this? Was it what he would want? It tore at her heart not to be able to ask him—an absence of the like the Wolkin rarely knew, and a deprivation that left her feeling hollow and weary.

"Perhaps we'll know soon, Frik," she said, around the leather-like strip in her mouth.

Presently, the orb of light began to resolve out of the mist; a rich, yellow glow, larger than it had at first appeared. She pushed the dugout on, the paddle scraping on the bottom of the swamp as she slid into an area of reed-choked shallows. She couldn't discern much through the mist, but she guessed she was close to another of the small islands that punctuated the swamps.

"Now, let's take a closer—" she stopped abruptly, clasping her hand to her mouth to stifle a scream.

The lantern was, as she'd suspected, a way marker of sorts—or perhaps a warning, raised to ward off any misguided folk foolish enough to venture near. The light originated from a large wax candle that had been placed inside the cavity of a human chest, cracked at the breastbone and prised apart, its soft innards scooped out and discarded. Inside, the jutting rib bones were blackened by the heat and soot, and what flesh remained clinging to them was now crisp and charred. Melted wax had run from the front of the opening, spilling down the corpse's distended belly in slick rivulets.

The naked body had been mounted on a wooden post sunk into the bottom of the swamp, so that the figure—the remains of a man, judging by the peeling, mouldering flesh—dangled above the waterline. Its feet were missing from the ankles, presumably chewed off by some aquatic monstrosity that had dragged itself clear of the surface to feast.

The man's face had been carefully removed, revealing the pale skull beneath. Just enough ligament remained to hold the lower jaw in place, fixed in a gap-toothed grin. The empty eye sockets stared ominously. Antlers—presumably taken from a young buck, had been forced through the skull's temples, which had been caved in by a blunt instrument of some kind. The upper branches of the antlers had been lashed to the top of the wooden post to maintain the corpse's ghoulish gaze; a tribute, Nok presumed, to the Kith's so-called god-who-walked-amongst-them.

Nok turned and spat the remains of the dry meat over the side of the dugout, her appetite gone. How many of these lights had she counted? Six, seven? And that was just what she'd seen through the mist. This was clearly how the Kith marked their territory—meaning she'd either strayed badly off-course, or the Kith had recently extended their reach. Either way, it was troubling.

"I think it's time we were going, Frik," she said, easing the dugout away from the gruesome figure and back towards the deeper water. If she paddled on until nightfall, she thought she might be able to clear the swamplands by midday the following day. Provided, of course, she was able to avoid the Kith.

The going was easier, now, and despite the apparent abundance of ropey weeds just beneath the surface of the water, the dugout glided easily through the swamp. Nok pushed on, gaining speed and momentum. The channel ahead was narrow, with arbaya plants crowding the verges and gnarled, leafless trees jutting from the uneven banks like crooked old men, stooping low to snare her as she passed. She dipped her head beneath the grasping branches, paddling quickly, the syrupy air forcing her to breathe harder and faster with the exertion. She imagined figures lurking in the shadowy spaces behind those trees, their eyes boring into her as she passed. It was fuel enough to keep her going.

After a short way the channel opened up again, and she paused for a moment, lifting the paddle out of the water while she caught her breath. Her palms were calloused and sore, and her back ached in a way it never had before. Yet the pain was preferable to—

Something tugged on the end of the paddle.

It was sharp and insistent—and strong, too—the wooden shaft was almost wrenched from her grip. Frowning, Nok peered cautiously over the side of the dugout, expecting to discover she'd inadvertently disturbed a nest of fiker eels that were now taking exception to her presence. Instead, she saw the paddle had become ensnared in a thick knot of reeds; black, sinuous things that had tangled around its flared end. She gave it a quick tug, trying to prise it free. In response, the reeds writhed like glistening snakes, tightening their hold on the shaft. She tried again, putting her back into it, but once again the reeds responded, retaliating with their own sharp jerk that, this time, had the effect of yanking the paddle from Nok's grip.

"What in the name of Wol?"

Dismayed, she watched as the weeds bubbled up around the marooned paddle, slithering over it until it was almost entirely obscured from view, before dragging it down into the murky depths of the swamp. Moments later there was nothing but a few bubbles on the surface to mark where it had been.

"Fuck!" Nok looked frantically in the dugout for anything she could use as a replacement. She was out of luck; aside from her bag of provisions, she'd brought nothing but her knife and the sack containing Frik. She'd have to go after it, risk lowering herself into the water to free it from the bindreed. Either that or swim to the shore to fashion a new one somehow.

As she started to push herself up, however, the dugout shifted suddenly beneath her, sliding forward as if shunted violently from behind. She toppled, unable to maintain her balance, upending into the boat and bashing her head sharply on the rim. She winced, pawing at her skull as she rolled onto her side, trying to catch her breath. It felt as if the world was moving.

Woozily, she sat up, still clutching the back of her head where it had struck the unforgiving wood. It was throbbing, needles of pain lancing deep into her brain. Thankfully, there didn't appear to be any blood.

Nok swallowed, steadying herself. She glanced back, half-expecting to see some tentacled monstrosity come clambering out of the water and up over the rear of the dugout... but there was no sign of anything there. She supposed the boat must have shifted beneath her weight as she'd tried to stand. But if that were the case, why did it still feel as if she was moving?

Frowning, Nok sat for a moment, watching the mist part before her like a wispy curtain. Branches loomed out of the grey to either side, only to disappear again, sliding quickly out of view. She felt disorientated, confused. She could hear something thudding wetly against the sides of the dugout.

Cautiously, she peered over the edge—and instantly recoiled. Beneath the boat was a writhing mass of the same black bindreed, slick and glistening like rotten entrails, rising out of the water to grasp the dugout and compel it along, driving it on towards some unknown destination. The dugout was gathering speed with every passing second, hurtling now across the surface of the swamp, so fast that she was forced to grasp the sides in white-knuckled panic just to remain sitting upright.

There was nothing she could do. If she jumped, she'd be caught up amongst the reeds, which, if they didn't immediately choke or drown her, would entangle her so completely that she'd be easy prey for any of the numerous predators that lurked in the foetid waters. With no paddle, she couldn't even fight back, or try to wedge the dugout against the bank. Her skinning knife was useless against such a foe. She was utterly helpless.

What in Wol was happening? What was compelling the bindreed?

Up ahead, the river formed a dogleg, kinking around the shore of another large island to disappear off to the left. But the dugout was heading straight for the verge. Worse, it was still gaining momentum.

On the shore she glimpsed movement amongst the fronds of the low-lying arbaya plants—little more than the shadowy outlines of figures, hazy through the gauze-like mist. Phantoms stirring, readying for her approach. *Kith.*

She reached for her skinning knife, sliding it out from the side of her boot, taking some small measure of reassurance from the feel of its wooden handle in her palm, worn and smooth.

And then the boat struck the verge with a sound like a detonation, and she was in the air, propelled forward with the momentum, turning heel over head as she crashed through the undergrowth and slammed down, hard, into the mud. Her body ignited in pain. She opened her mouth to scream, but the world around her was growing dim, as night closed in from all directions.

Everything went black.

Blood was seeping from the wounds at her wrists. It welled to the surface to form bright, glossy beads; tiny bloodbugs crawling up and down the pale skin of her forearms. She tried again to work her hands free of the bindings, but the rough twine had been knotted tight and bit deep into her chafed flesh, causing Nok to grimace in pain. She grunted, leaning back against the carved wooden post to which she had been bound.

She'd come to a short while earlier—head still throbbing from where she'd knocked it against the side of the dugout, ribs aching as if she'd cracked them in the ensuing crash—to find herself tied to the post in the middle of what she presumed to be a Kith encampment. Blind panic had been her first reaction, fighting against her bindings until the pain had finally cut through the fug of fear and rage, and she'd been forced to slump to the ground, breath coming in ragged, whistling gasps, wrists torn and bloody. The face on the carved post—a leering, stylised skull surrounded by a wreath of ivy—had seemed to laugh at her as she lay defeated in the slick mud, tears of frustration welling in her eyes.

That had been some time ago—perhaps an hour, perhaps longer—and so far, she was yet to see any sign of her captors.

The mist here was wispy and ethereal, drifting in translucent threads, and she'd established she was being held at the centre of a ring of small wood-framed buildings. The method of the buildings' construction was ingenious—two trees had been felled together to form an apex for the roof, a frame around which the rest of the structure had been erected. Presumably, these were the sleeping lodges or communal buildings of the Kith who were, she could only assume, responsible for her present situation. She'd know more when they deigned to show themselves, of course, but was in no hurry to make their acquaintance. The thought of them carrying her here, unconscious and insensate, made her skin crawl. Why was she still alive? Why hadn't they simply finished the job down by the water? And why had they left her to stew in the dirt for so long? Clearly, they had plans for her.

Behind her, she heard a sound akin to the rumble of distant thunder, only closer, like the breath of some stirring god, hot on the back of her neck—and felt her hackles rise.

She turned, craning her neck until her muscles burned with the strain. Heart hammering, she searched the gloom. She half-expected to find the god-who-walked-amongst-them looming over her, come to claim her as some sacrificial offering. But there was no-one, or nothing, there, save the wandering mist, clinging resolutely to the edges of the buildings.

Her heart skipped at the sight of a familiar burlap sack, resting by the door to one of the huts. "Frik?"

So, they'd carried him up from the dugout, too. For what purpose, she could only imagine, but the thought that his remains—or her own, for that matter—might be used in the crafting of one of those hideous way markers caused her stomach to turn over and bile to rise in her gullet.

Was that how this was going to end, this ill-advised adventure into the unknown? Is this what Trith-tree had wanted for her?

She knew that couldn't be true. Trith-tree had once been her mother, and despite the creeping entity that now puppeted her corpse, she remained, at least in part, the same woman who had fed Nok from her tit, had taught her how to walk, talk and wield a blade.

No, Trith-tree would not have sent her out here if she'd known what might happen. Unless she had faith enough that Nok had the resilience to see her way through it. Unless she believed that Nok would survive. The thought offered some small measure of comfort.

Yes, that was it. She was strong. She wouldn't allow them to break her, to violate her body or despoil Frik's bones.

"We'll get out of this, Frik," she said, surprised at the crack in her voice. "I promise."

"Who are you talking to?"

The voice was muffled, the accent clipped and unfamiliar. She craned her neck, chewing the inside of her cheek to stay the rising sense of panic. Her palms were sweaty, her fingers sticky with blood.

The man standing over her looked as if he had stepped out of the nightmarish unreality of a lyssan root vision. His face was a leering skull, emerging from a collar of ivy that was woven through with tiny, fragile bird skulls. He was tall, dressed in a mud-spattered cloak, beneath which he wore a stained leather jerkin to which he'd affixed an array of charms and totems, from bone fragments to wooden effigies, squares of faded parchment to silver wards. His hair was long and crow-black, and pulled back into a tight ponytail, knotted several times along its length. He carried a scabbarded sword at his belt, and the curved blade of a dagger in his left hand.

It was that skull face that most alarmed Nok, though—the pallid sheen on the skin, puckered and swollen around the edges of the mask where it had grown to accommodate the foreign object, absorbing it so that the bone had become a part of him, irremovable, permanent.

She had heard stories of the Kith rituals from the tree-kin. Horrible tales of how they would fashion the skull of their first kill into a gruesome mask, and then slice off their own noses as a coming of age rite, so that the mask might better fit over their face. Once there, it would never be removed, and as the child grew, the mask would become a part of them, a fixture, a new face, and they would adopt this new identity as their own. A killer. A warrior. A walking dead man. All this in tribute to their god-who-walked-amongst-them; a looming, bestial thing that demanded fealty in blood, that revelled in death and despair. The poison heart of their culture, beating out a rhythmic tattoo of suffering.

Now, she saw that it was true. Everything she had heard. The man towering over her was living proof of the horror of the Kith.

He was staring at her, his green eyes flicking back and forth behind the bone ridges of the mask-that-was-no-mask. "I asked you a question."

Nok swallowed. Her throat was raw. She could taste blood where she'd bitten through the side of her cheek. She wanted to whimper. But instead, she straightened her back in defiance, meeting his gaze. "No one," she said.

The man stepped forward and with one swift, sharp movement, backhanded her across the side of the face. Her head snapped to one side under the force of the blow, and she felt her cheek split. Her mouth filled with warm, gushing blood.

Nok allowed her head to hang for a moment, before slowly raising it once again to return the man's gaze. She spat a mouthful of blood on the slick mud between them.

"Who?"

Nok laughed. She was probably going to die here at the hands of these Kith. But she was damned well going to fuck with them in the process.

"My brother," she said, her lips curling in a bloody grin. "He's here, somewhere. Watching. Waiting. He's coming for you."

"Lies," replied the man. "You were alone when we dragged you from your boat. When the bloodweeds snared you and called to us. Just you and a bag of old bones."

"That's what he wants you to think," said Nok. "But you just wait. You've walked right into his trap. He's coming for you. He's going to prise that ugly skull right off your fucking face while you choke to death on your own blood."

Her head snapped back as the man brought his hand down again, harder this time. Groggily, she allowed the blood to dribble down her chin, splashing against the mud in stringy gobbets.

"Soon," the man said, his tone spiteful. "Soon you shall meet Utharat, and that smile will be gone from your face."

He turned and stalked away, disappearing into the wispy fog.

After a moment, Nok slumped back against the post, spitting the last of the gritty blood from her mouth. Her face was alight with pain, her left cheek split and already swelling.

Utharat. The poison god. The one who walked among them.

She was already as good as dead.

"Oh, Frik," she mumbled, through broken lips. "I'm sorry."

Chapter Six

'To live to excess is to bargain with devils. And devils recognise their own'
                    Brother Rodoric, Book of Remonstrance

THE SUN BEAT DOWN LIKE A BALEFUL EYE UPON the parched deck of the merchant ship, ever watchful, ever prying.

Deckhands milled industriously, carting innumerable barrels and crates down the gangplank to the stone jetty, and beyond that, the docks seethed with merchants and traders, beggars and whores, and all the other distasteful multitudes that characterised the great unwashed masses of humankind.

Ambrose shuddered at the very sight of it. Not to mention the smell. He wrinkled his nose, dabbing at his upper lip with the floral-scented kerchief he'd brought along for the very purpose of protecting his delicate senses from such demonic assault. The last time he'd visited such a place he'd nary fainted from the stench, and now, still somewhat queasy from the crossing, he feared it might happen again.

"Oh, to what bleak and fuliginous depths have I sunk to find my senses so assailed?"

"Come now, Arch-Brother-Imperialis—surely it is not *that* bad?"

Ambrose turned to regard the young man to his left, who—while evidently of an attentive persuasion—was clearly too young and inexperienced to understand the true measure of Ambrose's despair. It had been a terrible crossing from the mainland, characterised by tumultuous waves, groaning masts, drunken sailors and the most diabolical food that an Arch-Brother-Imperialis had ever been forced to bear. Gruel! Dried fish and strips of some ghastly grey meat, so salted as to resemble the mouthful of foul seawater he had inadvertently supped upon during his first night above decks, when he had stood too close to the railings at the stern and been utterly discombobulated by the backwash from a crashing wave. Much to his chagrin.

Seven nights, he had borne such burden. How he craved the taste of a mere honeyed fig, a sticky date, a sweet, buttery pastry melting upon his tongue. How he longed to return to his chambers and that soft divan, whereupon he might alight and dream of something other than the misery of bawdy sailors and rancid stew. How far he had fallen! How deftly he had been martyred for his cause!

He sighed and shook his head. The young scribe—Benedict, or Banfaeld, he couldn't *quite* remember—was scratching something down in his journal, quill whipping back and forth across the parchment as he studied Ambrose as one might observe a wild beast being held in captivity for the amusement of party guests.

"I see you are capturing this moment for posterity," said Ambrose, warily. "This most auspicious debarking of the famed vessel that has brought us thus far on our journey."

"Um, yes," confirmed the scribe. "Precisely that." His quill seemed to dance across the page in a final flourish, before the journal was slammed smartly shut, the man's stained fingertips leaving smudged impressions upon the leather cover. He looked up at Ambrose again, and grinned sheepishly. Ambrose sighed once more.

"Greetings of the day, Arch-Brother-Imperialis. Might I enquire if you are ready to be on your way?"

Ambrose turned to see a guardsman in a fine red coat standing before him, four thickly-thewed men in his wake. The man wore a tri-horn hat upon what appeared to be a full head of lustrous blond hair, and his whiskers were waxed to perfection, his beard sculpted into a neat, tapering point. A sabre hung from a hoop off his belt, and a small, golden brooch in the shape of a stallion's head was pinned to his lapel. Evidently, this was the captain of the Fauthian Guards who had been hired to escort Ambrose to the foot of the Broken Queen's tower.

"Humblest greetings, dear sir," said Ambrose, inclining his head in the shortest of bows. "I am, indeed, quite ready to take my leave of this most wretched of vessels. But first, if you'd be so kind, I would know the name of the generous saviour who comes so willing to my aid?"

"I'm sorry?"

"Your name, Captain," said the scribe.

"Ah. Of course. My name is Durant," said the man, touching two fingers against the brim of his hat. "Captain Saxle Durant."

"A most felicitous name," said Ambrose. "Now, if you would lead the way to our conveyance."

Durant stepped aside, and the four men, presumably also members of the carriage guard—although, Ambrose was forced to admit, somewhat lacking the refined airs of their illustrious leader—came forward bearing a large mahogany frame, which they laid upon the deck before them. Ambrose studied the object for a moment, taking note of the four wooden handles and the sheet of canvas stretched taut upon said frame. To his delight, one of the men beckoned him forward to take a seat.

Evidently, he was to be borne to the carriage upon a palanquin. He heard one of the sailors sniggering behind him but chose to ignore the offense; such men could never understand the subtle politics at work in such a delicate situation. If Ambrose were to refuse them now, would he not be undermining his very position? Would he not be starting out upon a slippery slope that would, over the course of the coming journey, erode the respect awarded him by the carriage guard? In turn, wouldn't such erosion place both him and his entire mission in grave peril?

False modesty, he had long ago learned, was not a virtue. By refusing the palanquin, he would be sending a signal, informing the guards that he was not worthy of such attentions. Thus, it was only the smallest of leaps before the men came to address him in a more casual fashion and, indeed—Pantheon forbid!—became overtly comfortable in his presence, spitting and hawking and scratching their groins. From there, one further step until they were entirely complacent—lackadaisical, even—deeming him "one of the boys", a man unworthy of their protection. Their guard would drop, and then—disaster!—the wildlings would strike, and all would be lost.

No, he could see it clearly now. He must uphold his position, for the good of the mission and the Order.

He lowered himself onto the palanquin.

The four guards shared a resigned glance, and then hefted him up onto their shoulders. Only one of them appeared to buckle under the weight.

———

The carriage was almost a temple in and of itself, raised in the worship of finery and gold. So large, and so brightly gilded, that Ambrose was forced to cup his hands around his eyes to look upon it.

Its wooden frame was the size of a large room, set on enormous axles, with six towering wheels to either side. It was lacquered in glossy black paint, with gold filigrees around the letterbox windows and swirling, golden inlays upon the doors. Above, behind the driver's box, was a roof terrace, where heaped, silken cushions had been arranged beneath a broad parasol. Neat iron railings ran around the edges of this terrace, serving as both a deterrent to any would-be assailants, and a barrier to protect those enjoying the pleasing space within.

At the head of the carriage, where Ambrose might have expected to see a small fleet of horses, was instead a hulking brown bear, shackled in leather harness and muzzle, its dusk-coloured hair worn patchy and thin. In general demeanour, the bear looked somewhat defeated, as if, in this act of domestication and humiliation, it had lost what had once defined it. Ambrose had seen the same happen to young men joining the Order, full of gusto and flamboyance, of ire and will. Slowly, over the ponderous months of that first year as a novice, such youthful vigour would drain away in a sluice of daily routine, prayer and song. A repetitive structure devised to erase all sense of individuality and ego. Death, Ambrose considered, by a thousand tiny cuts.

That said, the beast at the head of the carriage remained quite fearsome, and Ambrose decided to make a point of staying out of its way.

Huffing, the four men set the palanquin down upon the gravel—for they had carried the most grateful Arch-Brother-Imperialis several blocks into the harbour town, to the yard of a large inn, where the carriage awaited them. Throughout all of this, the scribe had walked alongside at a steady gait, scratching a stream of words into his journal. Ambrose would have to sneak a look at that little book, when the chance arose. If only to ensure that the man wasn't being *too* kind in his depiction of his saintly master.

With Ambrose duly positioned before the carriage, the four guards stumbled away, mopping sweat from their brows. One, Ambrose noted, did seem to be having some trouble with his back, and it occurred to him that the man mightn't be in the best of health, despite his impressive physique. It wasn't, he considered, an auspicious sign for a soldier.

"Here, Arch-Brother-Imperialis—allow me to help you up." This from Durant, who had gone ahead of the palanquin to ensure all of the necessary arrangements had been made. Ambrose smiled and offered his hand. Of course, he was quite capable of getting up by himself, but for appearances and all that...

"My thanks to you, Captain," said Ambrose, rising smoothly from the palanquin. He glanced at the inn, where the rear door stood open, and a man was rolling a fresh keg of ale in from the yard. The smell of stale beer wafting from inside was quite heavenly. The sign above the door depicted a mermaid in a state of undress—although Ambrose was uncertain if mermaids had ever been known for their modesty—wallowing amongst the shallows of some pleasant shore. Ambrose licked his lips. "Perhaps, while you make the final preparations, my scribe and I should await you inside the inn?"

"No need," said Durant, clapping Ambrose upon the shoulder. "All the necessary preparations have been made." He stepped forward and opened the folding doors. A boy—who couldn't have been more than twelve—scurried over and placed a set of wooden steps before the entrance. "If you'd like to step aboard..."

Ambrose glanced back at the inn and tried not to let his disappointment show. Graciously, he braved the steps up into the carriage.

Inside, it was furnished like an exotic boudoir, with a low table, heaped cushions and—Ambrose's heart soared—a plump chaise longue. Draperies hung from the walls, depicting scenes drawn from the great history of the Pantheon—Moshale defeating Obsidious during the Fall of Ithmont; Utharat raising his great army from the battlefields of the Dreg; Amaranth stirring from the ashes of her rebirth. Platters of sweets had been laid out upon the table, along with several decanters of fine wine. Sunlight streamed through the windows. A small desk had been propped in one corner from which Baledreth—or whatever his name was—could work.

It was a far cry from the horrors of the preceding few nights, that arduous week that had seemed to last an entire lifetime. No, this was far closer to what Ambrose had expected; to what he had become accustomed. This was a carriage suited to one of his standing.

Here, Ambrose was finally at home.

———

"Arch-Brother-Imperialis?"

Ambrose stirred, swatting at whatever it was that had tickled his face. "No, no. Stop that."

"Stop what?"

Ambrose frowned, opening his eyes. An unfamiliar face was staring down at him. He remained where he was for a moment, considering. There was definitely something familiar about the man. But what was he doing in Ambrose's bed chamber?

Clarity returned a moment later, and he levered himself up on the chaise longue, waving for the scribe to give him some room. Beneath his feet, the distant rumble of the road was a steady, background drone.

"You were snoring," said Ambrose, smoothing the front of his robes. He reached for the wine glass on the table and took a long, hearty swig.

"I was not!" said the scribe, somewhat indignantly.

Ambrose shot him a disapproving look. "Well, *someone* was." He shook his head, eyeing the scribe. Then smiled. He was in a forgiving mood. Well, it wouldn't do to disenfranchise the young man now, would it? "But that is of no concern. Have we arrived?"

The scribe shook his head. "Oh no, not yet, Arch-Brother-Imperialis. Indeed, we have several days of travel still ahead of us."

Several days? Trapped inside such a carriage, with little to do but rest and lose oneself in contemplation? "Oh dear," he said. "That *will* be a trial. Nevertheless, we shall endeavour to make the most of it."

"Quite so," said the scribe. "I have already completed several chapters of my latest book."

Ambrose eyed the man suspiciously. "Several *chapters?*" The man's productivity was close to legendary.

"Yes, indeed. I do find travel so inspiring. Don't you?"

"Oh, of course. Of course. Very *inspiring* indeed." Ambrose was beginning to wonder if the scribe was, in fact, a spy sent on behalf of the Prefect. Was *that* why he was watching every one of Ambrose's moves, jotting it all down in his little book? Enquiries would most definitely have to be made.

Irritated now, Ambrose quaffed another mouthful of wine, and then reached for a sugared plum. Oh, how he'd missed such treasures during his time aboard that despicable ship. "Well, what is it?" he said, after retrieving the stone from between his teeth.

"What is what?" said the scribe.

"What is the reason you wo—ah, disturbed my contemplation?"

"Ah, yes. A message from the Captain. He says that, although we are soon scheduled to make camp, he intends for us to carry on through the night. Dinner will be served in our…um…room."

Ambrose considered this for a moment. He disliked the notion of travelling on a full stomach—and worse, eating on the move—but needs, of course, must. "Did the Captain give his reasons?"

The scribe nodded. "Yes."

"Well?"

"Oh, right. He says we've entered dangerous wildling territory, and it would be ill-advised for us to make camp until we have reached safer ground."

"Then I should very much agree with the Captain's decision," said Ambrose. "He strikes me as a fine man of good breeding."

The scribe smirked. "Yes, exactly that, Arch-Brother-Imperialis."

Ambrose was reaching for another sugared plum—he needed to work up an appetite for dinner, after all—when the carriage gave a sudden, violent jolt, and he rocked forward in his seat, sending the entire bowl crashing to the ground, plums rolling off like tiny cannon balls across the wooden tread boards—along with a decanter of wine, whose contents glugged like spilled blood, draining away through the cracks in the floor. "What in the name of Hosst was *that*?"

Before he could answer, the scribe was sent sprawling across the floor as the carriage gave a second shudder, wheels screeching as it careened into a thunderous charge, bouncing across the uneven ground and setting Ambrose's jaw a-chatter.

A fist pounded on the roof. "Hold on tight in there. We'll try to shake them off."

"Shake them off?" echoed Ambrose, dragging himself to his feet. He clutched the back of the chaise longue as he tried to remain upright. On the ground, the scribe was scrabbling on his hands and knees for his book, which was sliding towards the back of the room like a wild animal trying desperately to escape its captor's grip.

Horses' hooves sounded outside like rapturous applause, galloping in pace with the carriage. Unsteadily, Ambrose crossed to a window, grasping hold of the scribe's desk—which was smeared in a slick of spilled ink—to steady himself. The view from the window made him giddy, as the carriage bounced over ruts in the uneven road, juddering up and down and presenting only the occasional glimpse of their would-be attackers.

Said attackers were up in their saddles, weapons drawn, closing in on the carriage at pace. They were not, however, simple wildlings bearing primitive stone bludgeons and wooden bows, but something entirely more sophisticated, and thus considerably more dangerous—renegade militia who had taken to prowling the trading lanes in search of wealthy prey to "unburden".

Ambrose ducked from the window as a wild bolt from a crossbow slammed into the frame, splintering wood as its iron tip burst through the panelling, inches from where his head had been only moments before. He glowered at it indignantly. He was supposed to be safe in here, protected by the Fauthian guards, to whom the Order had paid a not-insignificant amount in promissory notes. An amount, in fact, that Ambrose did not wholeheartedly relish disclosing to the Prefect upon his return to the monastery's hallowed halls. Indeed, following the settlement of said notes, the halls might be significantly less hallowed for some time to come. Yet what was he to do? The Question could only be put to Amaranth if he arrived at her tower in one piece, could it not?

Outside, swords sang from scabbards as the militia closed in. The air was rent by the deafening roar of the bear as it pounded the track, and, peeking through the window once again, Ambrose saw three of the militia go down, horses tumbling, flanks gouged, riders tossed like ragdolls across the hard ground. Clearly, his instinct had been right—it didn't pay to stray too close to that bear.

A thud sounded on the roof terrace above his head, followed by the ringing clash of blades.

"We've been boarded!" shouted the scribe, who was still on the floor, sitting now with his back pressed into the corner, knees drawn up, his precious book clutched securely in his arms.

"It appears so," said Ambrose, stepping away from the window. "Yet we must trust in Captain Durant and hi—" He stopped abruptly as the bloodied tip of a blade punched through the ceiling a few feet ahead of him, rude and startling, showering fragments of paint and wood upon the floor. The scribe screamed.

More thudding followed, as if describing the spasmodic kicks of a dying man, and then: silence.

For a moment the carriage rolled on. Then, with a low, rumbling growl, the bear began to slow to a more moderate pace, before the carriage finally juddered to a halt.

"There. It seems Captain Durant has already dealt with our interloper," said Ambrose. "It will be the matter of mere moments before the rest of their motley crew is expunged." He turned to the window to see a red-coated bundle slide past, strike a wheel, and thud to the ground like a sack of potatoes. The man's bloodied lips had made rather a mess of his previously well-coiffured moustache. A puncture wound, as of the type made by a plunging sword, was visible in his belly. His startled eyes were open and staring, his jaw hanging slack with surprise.

"Ah," said Ambrose. He swallowed, smoothing the front of his robes. "It seems my faith in said captain might have proved somewhat misplaced, after all." The scribe looked at him with an expression that spoke of deep existential terror. Ambrose shrugged. "Still, all good material for your opus, no doubt, hmm?"

He crossed to the carriage door, inhaled deeply, and then turned the handle, flinging the door open with gusto. There, staring up at him from the edge of the road, booted foot upon the bloodied corpse of one of the guardsmen who had borne him upon the palanquin, was a woman of the most startling appearance. Her dark-hued skin seemed to shine in the waning light, her green eyes bright and amused. She was dressed in a ragged old frock coat that had once been exquisite, but was now stained and worn around the hem, and in her hand, she held a rapier with as finely crafted a guard as he had ever seen. Her hair fell in long braids around her shoulders. She smiled at him expectantly.

Ambrose cleared his throat. "Felicitations of the day, my good lady!" He inclined his head in a low, appreciative bow. "Please, won't you come in?"

Chapter Seven

This blighted age
Shall be his burden
'gainst ancient foes
He stands as warden—
And walks

Whether beast or demon
God, or man
His blade in hand
He faces them—
And walks

He crosses oceans
Traverses realms
To seek his truth
'mongst gravest peril—
And walks

And walks

And walks

    The Ballad of Perisher Oswald, Traditional

"**We're being hunted.**"
  Stonn had stopped near the top of a shallow incline, looking down upon the sweeping monotony of the

forest behind them. The trees were thinning now as they climbed out of the depression, but the going was hard, the endless trudging through the snow drifts cold and demoralising. Pallor had awoken that morning to find his armour rimed in frost, the embers of the campfire cold and still.

Huffing, he made his way up the incline to stand beside her. He scanned the landscape, too, searching for whatever hidden signs she was seeing. To him, there was nothing but conifers stretching as far as the eye could see, their bristling upper branches dusted with powdery snow. Overhead, the sun was weak and hazy, lending an amber aura to what, Pallor considered, would have been a relatively pleasing scene—if it hadn't been so damned cold. Whatever Stonn had glimpsed, however, he could not see it. "We are?"

Stonn sighed, and once again, Pallor felt the stab of her disappointment like a blade to the heart. "The beast we hear by night. It follows us. It's probably waiting for us to tire, to make of ourselves easy prey."

Pallor waved a dismissive hand. "A single beast. We've seen off worse."

Stonn nodded but looked decidedly unconvinced. "Perhaps," she said. The look on her face sent a chill through Pallor that had nothing to do with their frigid environs. He turned, searching the horizon. There, in the distance, a few miles hence, was a stone-built tower, jutting from the earth like a broken finger. Its roof was misshapen, its walls crooked and leaning. It was the only habitation for miles in any direction.

"There," he said, pointing it out. "That must be it. The Broken Queen's keep." He grinned. "We near our destination."

Again, Stonn nodded, but her lack of confidence was infectious. Was this to do with her comments the previous night? Her attempt to dissuade him from this quest, to throw it in as a bad job and continue on to the nearest city. To abandon all hope of attaining his life's ambition amongst the ranks of his Brothers Perish.

In truth, he could not understand her reservation. Was it not a glorious aspiration? To die by a worthy hand, to undertake a pilgrimage through an underworld, to emerge again, remade—was that not a life well spent? What of that did she not want for him? What did she, a squire to such a hero, stand to lose? Surely, she, too, would bask in the glory of a quest attained. Yet for some reason her heart no longer seemed to be in it.

Still, there was little to be done about it now. The endgame was in sight. A god waited in that tower; a god who would smite him down and cast him into the netherworlds, from whence he would be reborn.

He beckoned to Stonn to continue on, setting out down the other side of the incline.

"What of the beast?" she said, as she stumbled after him, her feet kicking up clods of packed snow.

Pallor shrugged. "If it comes, we shall be ready."

"Says the man whose sword remains frozen in its scabbard."

Pallor reached for the weapon. "Not so, my dear St—" He hesitated, tugging on the hilt. It shifted fractionally but remained firmly wedged in the ebon and leather sheath. With a groan, Pallor released it. "I thought it was a squire's job to oil his master's weapons?"

Stonn shrugged and stalked past him, on into the snowy wastes ahead.

"The beast was here," said Stonn, kicking at the dead man's arm. Pallor scowled at such blatant impropriety. It was, after all, a human being she was kicking. Or rather, it *had* been.

They'd found the corpse—or rather, the *corpses*—a few leagues from where they'd last stopped to take in the view. Stonn had seen them first—the pink, frozen bloodstains in the snow, a trail leading off the path towards a small clump of trees—outliers from the forest, whose towering red boughs were now well behind them.

They'd followed the bloody trail to where it ended—it had seemed the only thing to do—and now, looking upon the grisly devastation that had awaited them, Pallor wished they had not.

The man, a pilgrim, perhaps, judging by what remained of his dress, had been eviscerated, belly ripped asunder by tooth and claw, so that the beast, whatever it was, might feast upon his glistening innards.

He was frozen, now, on his back, his body opened like a silk purse, blood frozen and glittering in the afternoon sun. His face was still intact, and the look of outright, primal terror fixed upon it was not one Pallor would easily forget. His eyes were open, but frozen over, dead white orbs, gleaming in their icy sockets.

Around the man were his companions in death; at least four of them, each opened up in similar, gruesome fashion, each seemingly *arranged* here, posed in some terrible diorama, their bodies now fixed forever in the diabolical throes of their deaths. Two had been hung from low branches in the trees, arms pinioned and skewered, heads lolling, like puppets whose strings had been cut but nevertheless remained tethered to their frames.

A further two had been placed in sitting postures, their backs to the same tree, their hands upturned upon their laps, as if they were cradling the remnants of their own viscera. These two had no faces left to speak of. Both appeared to be women.

Finally, there was the man, splayed upon the snow before them, his arms outstretched so that the tips of his fingers almost touched the feet of the two women.

Pallor had no notion of what the scene was intended to depict and was unsure that he wanted to. "No beast did this," he muttered. "This took planning, and *care*. The way these bodies have been placed—it's almost *reverential*, as if they're special, somehow. It's like some sordid tribute to an unknown god."

"Even beasts have gods," said Stonn, her voice level. "No human hand has touched this." She backed away from the dead man, surveying the rest of the scene. "It took them on the road, dragged them here while they were still alive, and fed on their innards. Then, before moving on, it took the time to *sculpt* them like this. Almost as if it were trying to thank them."

"Thank them? Damnable way of showing it," said Pallor.

"Beasts don't think like men," said Stonn. "At least, not in *most* ways." She eyed him with a crooked smile. "Perhaps it was grateful for a bountiful feast. Perhaps it *was* paying tribute to its god."

"And this is the same beast that's tracking us?"

"A hoarbeast, yes," said Stonn.

"How do you know of such things?"

Stonn laughed. "I am not as innocent as the world takes me for, milord."

Pallor was a long time in answering. "I see the truth in that, Stonn."

Had something changed between them, these last few days? Some imperceptible shift in the landscape of their relationship. Some redressing of a balance that had stood them in good stead for countless months, years. No longer were they simple knight and squire. And in revealing this hidden truth—which, now that he considered it, Pallor had suspected all along—she had altered that balance ever further. She had given voice to something that had, until now, remained unspoken. Not for the first time that day, Pallor felt as if he stood on uneven ground.

Stonn was sniffing the air. "It comes for us. It knows we're here."

"Then the sooner we get out of here, the better," said Pallor. "We can make the tower before nightfall if we hurry."

"No," said Stonn, folding her arms across her chest.

"No?"

"You have to kill it. We cannot allow it to get away with this." She indicated the bodies with a wave of her hand.

"A beast has no notion of punishment or revenge," said Pallor. "A beast simply *is*. As you say, it was probably grateful for the feast, and that is that. I do not relish being added to this spoil heap for the next unwary traveller to find."

"The beast must die," said Stonn. Her tone was intractable.

Pallor sighed. He could see that this was not an argument he was going to win. And besides, had he himself not stressed that the slaying of a beast was but a simple matter? Perhaps he had to give her this. Perhaps this was what it would take for her to let him go. "Very well. The beast will die. But first, I should examine the tower. If it proves to be the dwelling place of the Broken Queen, then I swear I shall not venture inside until the beast has been smited. If it is not, then at least we have a place of shelter for the night, from which to plan our next move."

Stonn nodded. "Very well. We're agreed."

Pallor rolled his eyes. "Well, I'm glad about that," he said.

The tower loomed out of the gloaming like a wizened washerwoman, stoop-backed and past its prime, no longer able to draw itself up to face the world.

Pallor could see now that it was beset by decay; the mortar had crumbled, and a whole half of the uppermost storey had sloughed away, exposing the jagged, broken beams like the ribs of a mouldering corpse. Birds flitted between cracks in the roof tiles, squawking their sad lament, or else laughing at Pallor and Stonn as they cautiously drew near. Snow had formed deep drifts against the outer walls, and yet, inextricably, fine, green moss had taken root, clinging to the slick stones, crawling over every surface like it was trying to drag the building back to the earth from whence it had come.

Pallor had the sense that the place had existed forever; an echo from another time, a hold-over from when the world had been inhabited by *others*.

"She isn't here," said Stonn. "This isn't her tower."

"Then what *is* it?" he said, circling the base until he found the door. It was rotten, hanging stubbornly off one rusted hinge.

"An abandoned home?" ventured Stonn. "An old barracks or guard post?"

"Guarding what?"

"Perhaps this used to be the gateway to somewhere affluent," said Stonn. "Like a whorehouse."

Pallor laughed. That was more like the Stonn he knew. "I'm going in," he said.

Hearing no objection, he drew his dagger—his sword was still frozen in its scabbard—and pushed the ruins of the door aside with his free hand. It creaked ominously and fell off its hinges, clattering loudly to the floor.

"Subtle," said Stonn, from somewhere behind him.

The ground floor of the tower comprised a single room, which had clearly been abandoned for some time. Centuries, in fact, judging by the thick layer of ice that had formed over every surface, glistening over an upturned chair, across tabletops and wall sconces, flagstones and curtains. It was as if the entire place had been flooded and then flash-frozen before the water had had chance to drain away. Even the shattered window had been glazed once again by a thick sheet of ice, giving the light a thin, watery texture.

Pallor's breath fogged as he crept further inside. The smell was musty, but somehow fresh, too, like the scent of a trickling spring. "What happened here?" he murmured, more to himself than to Stonn, who had crept in behind him and was now making her way over to the flight of stone steps that followed the inner wall up and around to the floor above. They, too, were thick with ice.

"I don't know," said Stonn, "but it doesn't feel natural."

Pallor was forced to concur. He'd heard tales of unnatural ice storms, of strange rituals, of underworlds spilling out like eruptions into the physical realm. Of Brother Knights who'd happened upon such things on their endless travels. He'd never imagined he'd encounter their like himself, however. If that was even what this was.

"Up here."

Stonn's voice echoed loudly from the floor above. He could hear her moving about, the ancient boards groaning beneath her weight. He followed her up the stairway, searching for a hand-rope but finding only perished strands where it had once been.

As below, this upper floor contained a single room, and here the ice had done its most devastating work. It was a bedchamber, containing the slumped wooden frame of a bed, a large, banded chest, and a desk. And sitting at the desk was the rigid form of a man, caught in the act of writing upon a scroll of parchment, quill still gripped between his fingers, brows still furrowed in deep thought. The ice had engulfed him utterly, capturing him in this perfect moment, preserving him in peaceful death.

Pallor crossed to the man, dropping to his haunches to take a closer look. He was young—no more than twenty—and hale, too; if it were not for the glossy layer of ice, Pallor could imagine him stirring back to life, turning to regard these newcomers with a welcoming grin. He wore a sword from a hoop on his belt—a weapon of the old style, with no quillon, forged from bronze rather than iron. A warrior, then—perhaps even a knight. His clothes were simple cloth, but Pallor could see the edge of a chain undershirt just visible around the neck. The words he'd been writing on the parchment were not legible beneath the ice.

"He's been here a long time," said Stonn, her voice barely above a whisper. "Centuries, perhaps."

Pallor nodded. "A curse."

"Or a murder."

He stood, stretching his weary limbs. "Neither thought fills me with relish."

"I don't suppose we'll ever know. The one who did this is probably long in the ground."

Pallor sighed. He turned to face her. "About this beast of yours, then."

Stonn shrugged. "It'll keep. Let's make camp. We can get a fire going downstairs, spend the night in relative safety."

Pallor grinned. "That's the best idea you've had in weeks."

She laughed, but the force of her punch to his upper arm made it clear that she wasn't amused.

Chapter Eight

The years did they pass,
And so the child, whose name was Aedle,
Did come of age,
And take up arms against the hated Children.
Through swamp and marsh, he strode,
Steeped in blood and vengeance,
And the Kith did quail,
And named him Quiet-Wolf,
For where he passed,
Naught but death lay in his wake.
   The Quietus Codex, attribution unknown

THE DARKNESS HAD SEEPED IN FROM ALL SIDES, like a fist inexorably closing around her, reducing the world to nothing but Nok and the wooden post, the twine and the blood.

There were puddles of it now, where she'd sawed at her binding until it didn't even hurt anymore, until she no longer recognised the pulpy mess of her wrists—but still she had failed to wrench herself free.

Nok sensed that the time was drawing close. The Kith warrior had spoken the truth. Soon she would face a god. Just not the one she had set out to find.

She was cold, shivering, damp with perspiration and piss. She had no idea how long she'd been like this. It might have been hours; it might have been days. She'd slept, briefly, fitfully, slumped in the mud at the foot of the post, no longer able to prevent her body from shutting down. She'd dreamed of the Greenwood, of Trith-tree and Frik, restored, melded with his chosen oak to take his rightful place amongst the tribe's dead. Yet, in the dream, Frik had seemed cold, distant—so unlike the brother she remembered and so desperately longed to see. She had reached out to cup his face, full of joy, and he had turned away from her, his expression blank, his tone scolding as he told her to leave.

She'd woken with a start, the shock of the wet mud and the pain in her bruised, swollen cheek bringing her round like a jolt of lightning. And then everything had come back to her, and she'd remembered where she was, and what bitter fate awaited her.

The Kith were gathering now—shadowy figures at the periphery of her vision, like ghosts amongst the gloom and mist, encircling her, impatient, hungry. Like predators awaiting a sign from their alpha that it was time for them to feast.

She thought to scream, to rail against the madness of it, the injustice, but her throat was parched and tight, and all that she could manage was a wracking sob, a sound so defeated and pathetic that she hung her head in shame.

They have reduced me to an animal. A primitive, frightened beast.

Somewhere in the distance a horn sounded—a long, droning dirge. A call to something ancient, something primal. Around her, the Kith began to murmur, a whispering susurration that reminded her, ironically, of the sound of the tree-kin, shushing slowly in the stirring breeze. It mingled with that distant dirge, growing in volume and intensity, reaching towards some terrible crescendo, towards a horrible fever pitch that seemed to quicken her pulse, to drown out all other thought.

She tugged again on her restraints, beyond desperate to free herself, to escape this oncoming terror. Around her a chill wind was rising, whipping her hair so that it stung her eyes, and she was forced to squeeze them shut, half in panic, half in pain. She clutched for the wooden post, clinging to it as the wind grew so fierce, so strong, that she felt her body buffeted, as if the wind itself were formed of slashing blades that cut so deep and true that her very soul might be severed from her body.

"Frik!" she called, screaming now, her voice lost to the unnatural storm, the incessant drone of the Kith and their terrible dirge. "I'm sorry, Frik. I'm so sorry."

The murmuring stopped. The wind dropped away, as suddenly as it had come. All around her was silent, as if the world were drawing breath.

This was it. The poison god was coming for her.

She squeezed her eyes shut; clung to the post that for so long now had been the thing that bound her, but now was all that she had left, her only remaining tether to sanity, to life. She wasn't ready. Not yet. Not like this.

And then the screaming started.

All around her, the Kith were bellowing in outrage. Something whistled through the air, close to where she knelt.

A crunch. A wet, sickly thud. Another scream. Boots running. Someone—a woman—groaning in pain. More whistling, as if arrows sailed through the gloom.

For a single moment, she wondered if her people had come for her—if the Wolkin had raised a raiding party and come in rescue—but she heard no war cries, no familiar voices, no clash of blades or chop of axe. And besides, who amongst them knew she was here? None but Trith-tree, who had sent her on this Wol-cursed quest.

Around her, the noises had stopped. All but the wet gurgling of someone close by trying to draw breath, their lungs burbling and steeped in blood. But she couldn't open her eyes, not yet.

Something brushed her cheek. Not a hand, nothing physical, but a breeze, an exhalation. Someone was there, standing over her. Someone who meant her no harm.

"Come, sister. It is time to go."

Her heart soared. Was it really *him*? She hadn't heard that voice in so long.

"Frik?"

She felt the bindings around her wrists slip free. She opened her eyes. There was no one there.

"Frik?" Frantically, she twisted, scrabbling to her feet, using the post for support. "Frik?"

But he was nowhere to be seen.

On the ground, close by, a wounded Kith lay on his back, gasping desperately for breath. His head was turned towards her, his expression implacable behind his hideous mask. Something jutted from his chest—something long and white.

She crossed to where he lay and looked down upon his wretched form. All around, others of his kind lay scattered, some dead on their sides, others groaning as they died, clutching at similar protrusions.

Nok dropped to one knee to examine the weapon more closely.

It was a human upper arm bone, mottled and yellowed with age. It had punched through the Kith's ribcage as if propelled like an arrow or a dart, collapsing his right lung and rupturing his spine.

She glanced around. The others were the same—wet, sucking holes punched through their chests, fragments of bone still buried in their hearts, stomachs, faces.

"Thank you, brother," she said, as she grasped the humerus and wrenched it free, causing the Kith warrior to spasm violently, hissing in pain, before growing suddenly, eerily still.

Nok reached for the sword that remained scabbarded at the man's belt, sliding it free, weighing it in her hand, feeling its balance. She rolled her shoulders, flexing her tired muscles. Then she turned towards the charnel field that had once been a Kith encampment, and *roared*.

A short while later she ran through the forest, errant branches whipping her face, arms, legs as she passed. In one hand she clutched the Kith warrior's stolen blade, still wet with the blood that also stained her clothes and spotted her cheeks. In the other, the burlap sack containing the bones of her dead brother, flung over her left shoulder—a heavy burden that, to Nok, felt light as air.

In the distance she could see snowflakes tumbling over the tops of trees, like blossom twirling in the sky, heralding the onset of Spring.

"It's all right, Frik," she said, amidst shallow gasps. "Everything is going to be all right."

Chapter Nine

'Only a life of infinite penance can prepare a man to meet his god. Only a life of infinite patience can prepare a god to meet his man.'

Brother Rodoric, Book of Remonstrance

THE TIP OF THE BLADE SCRATCHED AT THE DELICATE skin of his throat, causing a tiny bead of blood to well to the surface, reminding Ambrose that, given the circumstances, it would be very much in his best interests if he chose *not* to swallow.

"My dear, please—there is absolutely no need for such, um, lack of civility. I merely wish to discuss terms."

"And I *merely* wish to run you through and be done with it," said the woman, whom Ambrose had ascertained—through the stealthiest of means—was called Saranti.

Ambrose swallowed. Then reminded himself he wasn't supposed to be doing that. "I am a man of simple means," he said, in his most conciliatory voice, "and I present no threat to you or your men. Nor, I assure you, does my scribe." He glanced at the scribe from the corner of his eye. The man, who was still clutching his journal like a shield across his chest, nodded vigorously. "Please, lower your blade. It would be the work of but moments if, after we have spoken, you chose to raise it again in earnest. You might also see that I am unarmed."

The woman looked at him, and sighed. Reluctantly, she lowered her blade. Ambrose finally allowed himself to exhale. "I knew, upon first setting eyes upon you, that you were a most excellent judge of character. I extend to you my heartfelt thanks."

"Do not thank me yet, priest," she said. "You might yet find yourself serving as feed for that bear." She nodded towards the hulking beast that, still shackled to its harness and reins, had nevertheless rolled onto its side in the dusty road and appeared to be licking its paws.

"Truly, a fearsome beast," said Ambrose. And then hurriedly added: "the bear, of course, my dear. Not you. No, I should never equate a lady with such a base creature. Although I must add that you are, indeed, quite fearsome. If not a beast."

"What are we doing, listening to this fucking idiot," said one of the militia men, a swarthy-looking man who still wore the black military coat of his former regiment, the insignia long ago removed. Violently, if the tears in the fabric were anything to go by. Clearly the man had issues.

They were standing at the side of the road, the stationary carriage to their backs. Around them, the dead of the Fauthian Guard lay sprawled on the scraggy grass where they had fallen—a trail of broken bones and bloodied throats that marked the passage of the carriage. Ambrose tried not to look at them. Now was not the time for sentiment. Now was the time for pragmatism and, perhaps, a little flattery.

"I would, if you would be so kind as to consider it, like to set out for you a modest proposal."

"Let me guess. You propose that I don't kill you now and be on my way."

"No, no. Not at all." Ambrose considered for a moment. "That is to say, *yes*, indeed, but only in as much as it forms a prequel, of sorts, to a much more considerable proposition. A prerequisite, if you like."

"What makes you think I'd even be interested in a proposal from a man such as you?" said Saranti. He could see now that she was growing bored, her fingers twitching around the hilt of her sword. Beside Ambrose, the scribe whimpered.

"A man such as me? If by that you mean to say a charming, intelligent and—might I add—quite harmless man of a religious persuasion—"

"You didn't answer my question," she growled, cutting him off. Nearby, one of the others of her group had started going through the pockets of the dead guards. A most distasteful practise, Ambrose considered, although he decided it would be ill-considered to give voice to such an objection at this particular moment in time.

"Why, because you are evidently a woman of discerning taste," said Ambrose, pleasantly, trying to ignore the bead of sweat that was trickling, embarrassingly, down the side of his face. "And because I stand to make you very, very rich."

At this, Saranti offered him a broad, toothy grin. Ambrose tried not to recoil at the sight of the broken, yellow stubs. "Now, at last, you're beginning to speak some sense." She slid her weapon back into the leather hoop at her belt and spread her arms wide. "I think we should discuss this proposition over wine and a meal, don't you?"

"Oh, how wonderful," said Ambrose, allowing himself a little chuckle. "I do believe you're a woman after my own heart."

They sat at a folding table in the shade of one of the big conifer trees that lined the road. Nearby, the bear was still licking its wounds, and the rest of the militia had now cleared away the bodies of the deceased—mostly guardsmen, but with at least two of their own counted amongst them—for they had already begun to attract flies, and as a backdrop to dinner they served as a particularly unwholesome tableau.

Ambrose, still somewhat wary of the woman before him, reached for a pastry, which he placed delicately upon his tongue. He made an appreciative sound as he chewed it, before reaching for another. Honey dripped unnoticed from his chin.

"Tell me again why I shouldn't kill you," said Saranti, leaning back in her chair and propping her boots up on the table. What gruesome ichor dripped from the soles, Ambrose could not say, but his fingers danced away from any plates in the vicinity of the offending items, and he tried his best not to disclose his distaste. Beside him, sitting cross-legged on the ground, the scribe had once again taken to scratching away in his book. Saranti glowered at him. "Does he have to record *everything* we say?"

Ambrose smiled. "I fear it is his sole occupation, his very purpose in life. To rid him of it would be to render his entire being meaningless."

"A rapier through the throat would have much the same effect," said Saranti, pointedly.

The scribe slammed the book shut.

"Now, to answer your question more fully," said Ambrose, taking a sip of sweet wine (oh, how it cooled his sore throat and becalmed his thudding heart), "I must first admit to the gravest of errors."

"You must?"

"Indeed. For it seems I backed the wrong horse from the very beginning of this tiresome venture."

"You're a gambling man?"

"No one is more surprised than me, my dear, to discover that I am. Nevertheless, I spoke purely in the metaphorical. What I mean to say is, when I hired the honourable and now um...*retired* Captain Durant, I evidently chose unwisely."

Saranti shrugged. "I could have told you that."

"There is little need. You rather ably demonstrated said point through the effectiveness of your banditry. Which leads me to a further point."

"Which is?"

"That had I proved wiser or better informed, then I should, of course, have come to you in the first instance," he said, with a flourish. He reached for a glazed violet, and then decided against it, given their close proximity to the woman's boots.

Catching his evident displeasure, Saranti—whom, Ambrose had lately come to recognise, might yet prove reasonably comely, given a bath and a change of clothes... and some peppermint elixir—dragged her boots from the table and sat forward in her chair. Her expression had altered to one of frustration. "Come to me for *what?*"

"Why, to hire you, of course."

Saranti laughed. "You're right. You did make an error. I'm not for hire. Not for you, or anyone else."

Ambrose eased himself back in his chair, folding his hands across his ample belly. "My dear, it is my experience that *everyone* is for hire. For the right price, of course."

She narrowed her eyes. "And that price *is?*"

Ambrose waved airily in the direction of the carriage. "Well, clearly this fine conveyance and its most extraordinary beast of burden are already yours for the taking. But my Order, well—our vaults brim with riches beyond your wildest imaginings. Gemstones, precious metals, artefacts from eons past... Our means are without limit."

"Umm" said the scribe.

Ambrose waved him silent. "A promissory note could be arranged..." Saranti seemed lost in contemplation. "I am, after all, Arch-Brother-Imperialis..."

"And what would we have to do for this 'promissory note'?" said Saranti. "I ain't laying with you, if that's what you're thinking..."

"Pantheon be shamed! I am a monk, dear lady! I have taken vows."

"So had my father." Saranti took a gulp of wine. "If not that, then *what?*"

"Merely to provide an armed escort through these most treacherous of lands. My mission is of grave concern to my Order. I must reach the tower of Amaranth without delay. Just a few day's travel from here, I am reliably informed."

"The Broken Queen? What business might you have with her?"

"Why else would a man of my position undertake to visit a god? To petition her, of course! To lay a question at her feet and beg the answer. Nothing more, nothing less. And who better to protect my interests during said journey, but the exceptional specimen of womanhood who sits before me now?"

Saranti laughed. "I still ain't laying with you. But I'll take your coin."

Ambrose clapped his hands. "Most excellent news!"

"And be warned—I *will* collect my dues."

Ambrose swallowed, and glanced at the scribe, who was staring up at him in wide-eyed dismay. "I do not doubt it," he said, before returning his attentions to the table. He reached for a sugared plum. "Now, as we're to be partners, I do believe it's customary to celebrate such union with a feast!"

Chapter Ten

To die alone
Is all he craves
To seek a worthy
Route to grave—
He falls

The underworld
Shall be his path
Towards renewal
To defeat death—
He falls

The ages pass
Yet still, he roams
For death to him
Shall pass like storms—
He falls

He falls

He falls

THE BALLAD OF PERISHER OSWALD, TRADITIONAL

PALLOR STRETCHED TO TRY TO EASE THE CRICK IN his back. Everything being equal, it should have been the best night's sleep he'd had in a long while—camped safely within the walls of the tower, fire roaring, his belly full of rabbit—but instead, he'd spent much of it lying awake on his bedroll, turning over Stonn's words in his mind.

What had she meant to say, when she'd told him she was not as innocent as she looked? Was it yet another attempt to befuddle his mind and throw him off the course of his quest? Or was there more to it than that?

The night had passed in relative peace. After building the fire, he'd scaled the rest of the stone steps to the uppermost floor of the tower, where one of the walls had long ago crumbled, scattering debris across the flagstones. Here, the unnatural ice had seemingly given up, leaving the ruins exposed to the natural elements, and therefore subject to the entropy that assailed all things, over time.

Looking out, he'd seen another tower in the distance—a keep of similarly ancient provenance, just a few leagues away—and knew this time that he was close. Amaranth stood in that tower, most probably gazing out just as he was upon the frigid landscape, tinted blue by the pale glow of the moon.

He'd returned to the lower chamber to find Stonn preparing the meal, and had settled in beside her, comfortable in one another's company and finding a welcome, companionable silence. Later, she had asked him to recite a tale of the old Brother Knights, so he had told her of Effinger the Graven and his perilous journey through the caverns of Hysst, and the bargain he had struck with a demon to return to the physical realm, scoring his name on the demon's heart as a means of binding their souls. Sooner or later, Effinger knew, the demon would call in its favour, and the knight would be beholden to return to the underworld in its place, so that the demon might taste freedom of its own. Of course, this had all taken place in ages past, and the story of what had eventually become of Effinger had long since been lost to posterity.

Pallor hoped, on hearing such a tale, that Stonn might better understand his own desire to undertake such a quest. If she did, however, she spoke nothing of it.

Now, all thoughts of quests were far from his mind, as he took a piss against the outside wall and contemplated breakfast. He would need a full stomach if he were to go up against a god that day. No one, he believed, should ever face death on an empty stomach.

Such musing was cut short by the low baying of some nearby animal, a sound so instinctively terrifying that it caused his steaming piss to cease midstream and his guts to tremble. It was like nothing he'd heard before; a flat, sonorous howl that might well have been a warning call, if he didn't already know that the beast to whom it belonged had no intention of warning him off.

"Fuck!" Hastily, he buttoned up the front of his breeches. His armour and his weapon were still inside the tower. He'd been a damned fool to wander out here unprepared. "Stonn! I think your beast is here…"

He could hear its trudging footsteps now, drawing ever closer. He could see nothing around the other side of the tower base, and given the sounds the thing was making, he wasn't at all sure that he wanted to.

"Stonn!"

"Here!" He turned to see her standing in the open doorway, his scabbarded sword in her hands. She winked, and tossed it to him, before pulling her own short sword from her belt.

"You stay inside," he said, drawing his blade and throwing the scabbard aside. "I'll see to this."

"Whatever you say," she replied, edging out of the doorway and circling around to the other side of the tower.

"Stonn!" He shook his head and hurried around to join her.

She was standing with her back to the tower, sword arm extended, trembling at the sight of the beast that was regarding her from about a hundred yards away. Even from here, he could see the intelligence in those lambent eyes, the way it was weighing them both up, carefully assessing its next move.

This is a beast that knows of gods.

It was as hideous a creature as Pallor could ever have imagined. It resembled an oversized elk, with a red, shaggy coat of hair and two massive horns erupting from its head, so weighty that its neck was bowed beneath their sheer size. Its torso was bulky and muscular, its four limbs terminating in immense hooves. It was the creature's mouth that most appalled Pallor, however—a lamprey-like ring of vicious-looking teeth, encircled by a monstrous array of writhing tentacles, grey and slimy, like dangling worms that had buried their heads in its jaw as if trying to burrow deep into its face.

Pallor raised his sword. He had no idea how he was going to fight the thing, let alone kill it.

The hoarbeast blinked, lowered its head, and charged.

"Move!"

Pallor shoved Stonn to the right as he dove in the opposite direction, breaking into a roll, flensing skin from his left shoulder as he skidded across the glassy surface of the ice. He grimaced, forcing himself up just in time to see the creature slam into the tower wall where he'd been standing, unable to alter the trajectory of its charge.

The wall crumpled beneath the force of the impact, the whole side of the tower slumping, hunks of masonry and shards of broken ice raining down in a thunderous cascade. They fell upon the creature's back, shrouding it in a billowing cloud of dust.

Even under such tremendous punishment, however, the beast was not dissuaded as, grunting, it raked its horns through the debris, pulling its head free from where it was buried in the collapsing wall, bringing hunks of stone and ice along with it.

It staggered back, shaking itself groggily, and then turned toward Pallor, its mouth irising open in a terrible, mangled roar.

Frantically, Pallor searched the ruins. There was no sign of Stonn.

He had no time to call to her before the creature was upon him again, hooves scraping the ice as it charged. He could feel the rumble of its every step through the soles of his feet, as if the earth itself was responding to the presence of this strange and violent thing.

Pallor raised his sword, standing his ground. The beast was only seconds away. The momentum alone would be enough to kill him, crushing his body like a witch's poppet made of sticks and straw. But now was not the time to die. Not if he could help it.

The hoarbeast dipped its head. Tentacles whipped out like lashes. Pallor swung his blade as he side-stepped, dancing neatly to the left as the creature bore down on his position, deftly dodging the rending tip of its immense horn as it roared past.

Blood sprayed, showering him as several of the creature's tentacles struck the ground, still writhing and twitching at the sudden severing of their nerves. The stink of the thing was breath-taking, like rotten carrion and festering shit. Pallor scraped its blood from his eyes with his fingers.

Raging, the creature swung its massive neck, catching Pallor off-guard, so that the flat of its horn struck him hard across the back with such force that he was lifted from his feet and thrown back towards the ruined tower, where he collided with a remaining stub of wall and slid, groaning, to the ground.

His lungs burned, gasping fruitlessly at the air. His skinned shoulder was on fire, and he was certain he'd cracked some ribs in the collision. Yet he had no time to dwell on it, as the beast was already rounding for another charge.

Hacking, Pallor stumbled to his feet and snatched up his sword. His head was throbbing and the world seemed to spin. Blackness limned his vision. He shook himself, forcing air into his lungs, raising his blade.

This hoarbeast, however, could see that he was done. *Already*. It paced for a moment, sniffing the air, regarding him with those strange, keen eyes. Like a cat, toying with its kill.

What sort of knight am I, that I cannot even face down a beast? He'd hardly even wounded it. His sword arm wavered. The beast moved in.

Pallor launched himself forward to meet it, swinging his blade in a wide, swooping arc, bellowing the names of his Brother Knights.

"For Caverus! For Jordath! For Stonn!"

The beast twisted, rearing up on its hind legs, angling its head so that Pallor's blade clanged harmlessly off its horn, the reverberations causing his arm to spasm, so that the sword spun uselessly from his grasp.

That strange, demonic mouth blossomed open before him, revealing the pink flesh of its gullet, lined along its full extent with rows of saw-like teeth. Tentacles—some of them still dripping with pulsating blood—coiled around his limbs, his waist, his throat, ensnaring him utterly.

The creature's front hooves crashed back to earth, cracking the icy mantle, as it hoisted Pallor up into the air amongst its writhing nest of proboscis, regarding him as one might regard a hunk of meat on a spoon.

He struggled, tried to wrench his arms and legs free, but he was caught fast, unable to gain enough leverage to break away from the tentacles' oily grasp.

Perhaps, Pallor considered, this was his time. Perhaps in this beast he had finally found that most worthy of foes, the mortal enemy that would deliver him to the underworld, from where he might begin anew. Perhaps he did not need to face a god to achieve his Perishment, after all.

He clenched his jaw, refusing to give the beast the satisfaction of crying out as it dragged him inexorably towards that terrible maw.

He sensed movement in his peripheral vision and angled his head just in time to see something—Stonn!—seemingly drop out of the sky. She landed heavily on the hoarbeast's back, grabbing fistfuls of its woolly hair to prevent herself from sliding off. Her short sword was clenched between her teeth.

She must have been lurking all this while out of sight, clinging to the upper levels of the ruined tower, waiting for her moment to strike.

Nimbly, she scrambled over the creature's broad shoulders as it bucked and twisted, trying ineffectively to shake her off.

Pallor, still clutched tight in its coiling grip, was thrust violently from side to side as it fought, whipping his neck back and forth painfully, but to no avail, for within moments, Stonn had the thing's neck squeezed tight between her thighs.

She flashed the briefest of smiles at Pallor, before carefully taking the short sword from between her teeth, angling the blade at the base of the creature's skull, and jamming it forward with a shunt from the heel of her right hand.

The blade slid under the bone with a sickening crunch, severing the beast's spinal cord and plunging deep into its brain. It issued a final, high-pitched wheeze, took a single step to the left, and then its legs buckled from underneath it and it slumped heavily to the ground.

Pallor collapsed amongst the nest of slimy tentacles, still twitching and curling and sliding hideously over his skin. He dragged himself free and clambered to his feet.

The creature's eyes had already lost their lustre, as if whatever light had once lived inside it had fled, leaving behind nothing but the inanimate hulk of muscle and dead flesh.

Grinning, Stonn retrieved her blade, wiped it clean on the beast's flank, and came around to stand beside him.

"Another conquest," she said, nudging him with her elbow. "We're getting good at this."

Slowly, Pallor turned to regard her beaming face. He stooped to retrieve his sword. "Yes," he said, wearily. "I suppose we are."

Still smiling, Stonn made a beeline for the tower. The doorway was leaning alarmingly, and a large section of the wall was missing. She paused on the threshold to look back at him, still standing before the corpse of the massive beast, dripping in blood and ichor. "Come along, milord. You'd better think about getting dressed if we're going to keep your appointment with that god today."

He watched her disappear into the gloomy building. And laughed.

Chapter Eleven

'Thus, the servants of the Broken Queen did gather, and the threads of her web pulled taut.'
SATER JON, ON THE CURSE OF EVER-LIVING

"We're here, Frik. We made it."

Nok carefully set the burlap sack down on the snowy hillside and slumped to the ground beside it. Her breath plumed. She was sweating, despite the cold—she'd run for the last few miles, plunging ahead through the dawn light after emerging from the cover of the forest to find herself entering a pure, white world. She'd never seen snow quite like it—what snow fell upon the Wolkin village was soon trodden to mush, turned filthy from the mud and the ash from the fire pits. Here, though, it was crisp and bright and clean, unmarred but for the passing of birds or the occasional fox.

She'd been running for days. She'd lost track during her flight through the woods—or rather, she hadn't seen the significance in caring. Day became night became day, and all that had mattered was her survival, and getting Frik here, to Amaranth's keep.

She was still grimy with blood, despite her efforts to wash it off with handfuls of snow, and her wrists—now bound in rags she had torn from her clothing—still throbbed with every movement, every gesture.

The Kith had only pursued her a short way into the forest before breaking off, although she had kept up her pace, still concerned that a small party of trackers might yet strike out to follow her trail. The devastation she'd left in their settlement would demand answer—of that she was certain. That, though, was a problem for another day. She would allow herself this small moment of triumph—sitting here, on this frozen ridge, overlooking the listing, crumbling keep of the Broken Queen.

Now that she was here, though, she wondered what might face her on the other side of that wall. Would Amaranth even permit her entry? And could she really dare to hope that the god might hear her petition and, more, that she might deem her worthy and restore her brother after all this time?

Nok had had a great deal of time to consider what had happened at the Kith encampment, yet she was still none-the-wiser.

I heard his voice. As clear as I can hear those birds singing. As clear as if he'd been standing right there before me.

Had it been some kind of manifestation? Had he risen from the underworld to come to her aid? The idea seemed incredible. She'd heard stories of ghosts, of course—uneasy spirits that refused to rest, that blighted the lives of their former loved ones, giving no quarter, offering no reprieve from their eternal torment. But this—it was different. He hadn't come to torment her. He'd come to save her. And then he had gone again, as swiftly as if he'd never been there at all.

She thought she might have dreamed the whole thing, if it hadn't been for the injuries she'd sustained, the Kith sword at her belt, and the bloodstains on her face and arms—stains that she now feared were indelible.

No. It happened. He was right there.

Would Amaranth judge her? Would she ever stop judging herself? These were the questions that haunted her more than any ghost. She supposed there was only one way to find out.

With a groan, Nok levered herself up to her feet, dusting the snow from the back of her legs. Then, weary and afraid, she hoisted Frik onto her shoulder and ambled down to the keep.

The crooked entrance yawned before her, silent and bristling with shadows.

She patted Frik with her free hand, puffed out her chest, and walked in.

Parting from the woman whom Ambrose had, lately, come to consider the most *delectable* Saranti was, it transpired, something of a bittersweet irony.

It was a long held belief of the Arch-Brother-Imperialis that proximity bred familiarity, and from there, the path between two people forked, leading on towards either contempt (the present state of his relations with the Prefect were a perfect indicator of such—not to mention his newfound weariness with his so-called scribe), or, indeed, affection. And affection was what had clearly burgeoned between Ambrose and the woman who had adopted the mantle of his personal guard.

Of course, she had spent much of the journey—all of it, really—in denial of said truth. But wasn't *she* the one who daily raised the subject of carnal relations? Yes, she would argue, it was simply a matter of reminding him of the rules she had stipulated at the very beginning of their affair—which, he begrudgingly admitted, had been a *business* affair—but surely it was not normal to speak of such things so freely, and indeed, so frequently. The woman clearly had sex on the mind. And now, of course, Ambrose could think of little else.

Not that he would ever deem to break his promise to a woman. He was, if nothing else, a man of his word, so while he had taken to gazing longingly at the object of his flowering affections, he had not, under any circumstances, initiated anything even resembling physical contact. Unless her repeatedly threatening him with her rapier counted as such—his throat was really quite sore—but he had learned to accept that as a sign of her ongoing frustration in the face of their unconsummated bond.

Oh, such precious love! How I hate to defy our destiny. To stand resolute on the precipice and refuse to contemplate the leap. Such is the strength of my word, my belief.

He was a man of his vows, and despite her obvious desire for their relationship to become more, he would stand by his Order, and she would be forever disappointed.

Much as he had been, when she'd effectively shoved him from the carriage at the base of the tower, along with the scribe and their travelling cases, before hot-footing it off into the distance, yelling that she would be seeing him soon enough to call in her debt.

It was not, as Ambrose had imagined, the parting of two great loves torn asunder by circumstance—but had she not at least promised she would see him again? His heart could nary wait.

"How are we going to get back to the monastery after we're done here?" said the scribe, who was looking at the snowy wilderness with a forlorn expression which might have been almost comical, if he had not had a point.

"Baeron—we stand here on the verge of greatness. Are we not mere moments away from kneeling before the beatific benevolence of a god? Are we not about to bend history itself to our will, with such a bold and courageous step towards enlightenment? Will our names not be heralded in song across the great nations of the world? And you—you deem to worry about a triviality such as our conveyance?"

"Beni—"

"No, no!" I shall hear no more of such mundanity."

"But that's not my name. It's Beni—"

"Ah-a! A scribe's place is to record, is it not? To make oneself invisible to the reader. To hide behind the curtain of others' words and bear witness to the unfolding of events so that others might borrow your eyes."

"Well, I suppose so," said the scribe.

"Then, dear scribe, I suggest you fetch out your quill. For the time is nigh. We venture to our fates."

"Our *fates*? She's not going to *kill* us, is she?"

Ambrose paused. "Only if you continue on in such dreary fashion," he turned to regard the scribe, "and only if I do not take measures into my own hands first."

The scribe swallowed and pulled his journal from a fold of his robes.

"Come, now. Let us get out of this interminable cold. Lead the way."

"I thought my place was to record. To hide behind the curtain of words. It looks dark in there."

"Oh, great Pantheon," said Ambrose, looking to the sky. "Why should you curse me in a such a way? Is a broken heart not enough of a burden to bear?"

"A broken heart?" The scribe was hastily searching for a blank page, quill poised at the ready.

"Just get inside," said Ambrose, taking him by the scruff of the neck and dragging him towards the entrance.

"I ask again—are you certain this is what you want, milord?" Stonn crouched by the base of the keep, examining the tracks in the snow. "It seems there are...others here, too."

"Then there is little time to waste. I must face her, Stonn." Pallor, still smarting from the battle but now attired in his full suit of armour, had his back to her, facing the gloomy passageway beyond the entrance.

"Your mind is made up, then. You're really going to go through with this. You're going to challenge a god to a fight."

For a moment, Pallor felt his resolve begin to slip. Did the woman have *that* little faith in him? He turned to face her, to find her standing right there behind him. "The purpose is not to *win*, Stonn. Surely you know that by now."

"I know," she said. She was refusing to meet his eye.

"Then you think me a coward? That I might shy away from the conflict to come? I might show my true face to the world, and be found wanting?"

She looked up then, her eyes bright in the glare of the morning sun. "Quite the opposite, milord. I believe that you will face her with a smile on your face, and honour in your heart."

"Then why do you question me so?"

She hesitated. Then looked away. "I suppose I've grown used to your company. And I've still got so much to learn."

"Pah! Not if the way you handled that beast this morning is anything to go by. You put me to shame."

"No, not that. Never that."

He paused, searched her face for some sign of what she really meant to say. She looked far older than her years. There was wisdom there, written in the soft lines around her eyes, the creases around her lips. He felt a sudden pang that he might never look upon her face again. "I do believe the future holds great things for you, Stonn."

She nodded, but her lips remained tightly pursed.

"But you've had enough of my platitudes. Come along, let's finish what we started all those years ago."

She shook her head. "You go ahead."

"And you'll follow?"

She turned away. "I'll wait here."

"Stonn—"

"I can't…"

They stood for a moment in silence, neither meeting the other's eye. "I understand."

He hesitated for a moment longer, and then turned and walked into the gloom.

Amaranth was standing by the window when Sleath entered her chamber, holding precisely the same pose as she had when he'd seen her last. He wondered if she'd moved in the intervening days, if she even truly existed in this form when he wasn't in her presence. He didn't suppose he'd ever know. He cleared his throat to announce his arrival.

She turned to regard him with her strange, fractured eyes. "You've not had time to see to your legs."

He shrugged. "It'll give me something to do in the centuries to come."

"Oh, I don't think it'll be that long. Not this time." Her voice was airy but threaded with something hard as steel.

That's what you always say. But perhaps this time you mean it.

He could sense the changes coming. The subtle shifts in the currents of the world. Things would be different after this.

"They're here." It was a statement, not a question. She'd seen them from the window as they'd converged upon the keep that morning.

"Yes, mistress. They're each of them wandering the halls. As proficient as they are, I don't suspect any of them will be able to breach the maze."

Amaranth's lips twitched. It might have been the beginning of a smile. "Well then, dear friend—what are you waiting for? Go, go and welcome our guests."

Sleath felt something break. For the first time in centuries, it wasn't a piston or worn joint. He dipped his head in a short bow. "As you wish." He turned back to the door, then paused on the threshold.

He was about to speak when Amaranth cut him off. "It is necessary, Sleath. All of this. They must understand the truth. They must see it for themselves."

"As you say." He started down the passageway, legs creaking loudly with every shift in weight. When he glanced back through the open door from the other end of the passageway, Amaranth had returned to gazing out of the window at the wintery scene below.

Chapter Twelve

'Life, it transpires, is ever Amaranth's curse, for to be eternally reborn, she first must eternally die.'
SATER JON, ON THE CURSE OF EVER-LIVING

H**E FOUND THE FIRST OF THEM WANDERING THE** halls of the vertical maze that comprised the lower levels of the keep.

Here, the passageways and chambers followed crooked paths, like the fracture lines that traced patterns through his mistress's eyes, kinked and uncertain, altering one's perception of the world. To navigate them was to walk the broken mind of their creator.

She started like a cornered animal as Sleath approached, tugging at the pommel of the stolen sword at her belt, eyes wide and fearful. "Come no closer, demon" she said.

She was weary now, this pilgrim; a savage girl, spattered in old blood.

Old blood.

Now there was an irony. He could see the ancestry etched in the line of her jaw, the slope of her nose, the colour of her hair, her skin. She belonged to another time, when the teeming forests spanned the world and the god-beasts knew nothing of humankind and its troublesome patrons. Simpler days.

He paused, his worn joints sighing in relief. "Fear not, child. I am armed with naught but welcome words. Amaranth sends her greeting."

She stared at him in sudden understanding, yet her fingers still danced across the hilt of her sword. "*You* are the Broken Queen?"

Sleath laughed. "No, no. I am but a humble servant, like you. My name is Sleath. And yours is Nok. The mistress would bid you come with me while we await the others."

"There are others?" said Nok.

"Of course," said Sleath. "There are always three."

"I don't understand."

"You will."

Nok bristled. "If you try anything…"

"You will cut me down. Yes, yes. I do not doubt it. But then where shall you be? Lost in a confounding maze you might never solve, and with an angered god at its heart, pining the loss of her beloved servant."

Nok seemed to consider his words. "You'll take me to her?"

"All in good time. She is anxious to make your acquaintance."

"Very well." She nodded her assent. "Then I shall follow you."

"Good, good," said Sleath. "This way." He turned on creaking limbs and set out again in the direction from which he had come. After a moment, she followed, remaining several paces behind.

He led her through a narrow passage that might have been nothing but a shadow on the wall, down a sloping hallway with a lopsided roof, and up a spiralling staircase that opened onto a large room draped in tapestries. They were faded now—barely visible—but once they had depicted all of human history and beyond; from the shaping of the underworlds to the wars that had once blighted whole continents and would again.

In the centre of the otherwise empty room, a small table had been laid out, piled high with jugs of wine and platters of roasted meats. Nok eyed them hungrily.

"Go ahead," said Sleath. "Eat, drink. The next of our guests will be along presently."

Cautiously, Nok approached the table. She grabbed a handful of meat and sniffed at it dubiously. Then, unable or unwilling to fight against the raging hunger she must have felt after days of eating scraps in the forest, she fell upon the feast, gulping down successive fistfuls. All the while, she stubbornly refused to let go of the burlap sack that was slung over her shoulder. Sleath smiled. In this one, Amaranth had chosen wisely.

A footstep sounded by the stairwell.

Sleath turned, slowly—for any faster and he risked popping a hip—to see a tall man standing on the top step, dressed in a suit of tarnished armour and clutching a bloodied sword. His face was scarred and dirty, and he stood with his weight on his right foot, suggesting he carried an injury he would not otherwise disclose.

Ah, the knight.

"Welcome, Sir Pallor. Please, join us."

Pallor's expression hardened. "I'm here for the Broken Queen."

"Aren't we all?" said Sleath, with a placatory gesture. "Now, lower your weapon. If you truly are a knight of virtue, then patience is what you must demonstrate now."

"Who are you? How do you know my name?"

"I am Sleath, a mere servant of the one you seek. And I bid you welcome. The answer to your latter question should perhaps be self-evident. Amaranth is all-seeing, after all."

Pallor made a grunting sound but lowered his sword. He did not return it to its scabbard. "And this? Who is this?" he indicated Nok with a nod of his head. She, in turn, was watching him nervously, as if expecting him to lash out at her at any moment.

"Another pilgrim, come to petition the Queen."

Pallor frowned. He stepped into the room. "What is this? You act as if I was expected. As if I am but one of several come for Amaranth this day."

"And so it is," said Sleath, with a broad grin. "It is a hard lesson, is it not, to learn that one is not special or, indeed, unique? And yet here we are, awaiting the final guest of this esteemed convergence."

"Three, then," said Pallor, nodding, as if weighing his thoughts. He eyed Nok, taking in the dried bloodstains on her face and hands, the weapon at her waist. "So you, too, seek to join in ba–"

Bickering voices from the stairwell drowned out his final words.

"–no, no. You are wilfully choosing to misrepresent my words."

"You misunderstand me, sir! I am merely a scribe. I record facts, nothing more, nothing less. If the words are inscribed in my journal, then they are the words that were spoken. Verbatim."

"Facts—pah! Hardly the stuff of poetry and song! Tell me, when last did you witness a bard enrapture an audience—an *unforgiving* audience—with a performance of the purest *facts*?"

The two men rounded the top of the stairs. Silence descended.

"Arch-Brother-Imperialis," said Sleath. "Good of you to join us."

"It seems," said the scribe in a hoarse whisper, "that we are late."

"But for what, dear scribe? For what?" Ambrose studied Sleath for a moment, then took in each of the others in turn. "A wildling!" he announced, upon setting eyes on Nok. "How...unexpected."

Sleath rolled his eyes.

"I gather, then, that I am not alone in seeking audience with the estimable and, might I hope, benevolent god that resides within this keep?"

"Correct," said Sleath.

"Ah, the strange and unfathomable minds of the gods. It has forever been thus. To such beings, dear scribe, we are naught but playthings; counters to be moved around a chequered board at their whim."

The scribe began scratching in his journal with his quill. Ambrose smiled.

"Indeed, to see the world through such vivid eyes is to—"

Sleath coughed, cutting short the verbose soliloquy. "If you're ready?"

Ambrose looked suddenly taken aback. He smoothed his robes. "Quite ready."

"Then Amaranth will see you now." Sleath reached for one of the tapestries—a faded depiction of a dying man-beast, felled by the sword of a Nysskan warrior—and tugged it aside, revealing a small opening in the wall behind. The rotund priest would, he decided, just about fit through. "This way," he said, urging them on. "She's waited long enough."

Amaranth sat upon a broken throne, two halves of sheared obsidian that, despite the fracture that ran through their very heart, was without doubt the most exquisite piece of sculpture Sleath had ever seen. Its tall back was crested by a depiction of the spheres, circling orbs of varying size that seemed to dance and revolve in the spear-like shafts of light that fell from the cracks in the ceiling. The arms were roaring lions, so lifelike that, in the gloaming, Sleath almost wondered if they might stir to life, commanded by the god to prowl the silent shadows of the keep while she slept. The seat itself was hewn in two, but it was as if the crack had forever been a part of the intended design, symbolic of the duality of Amaranth's existence—the division between night and day, life and death.

The throne stood upon a dais at the end of a long hall, itself divided by a parade of towering statues, each of them to some degree broken or defaced, missing limbs, heads or even torsos; relics, Sleath knew, from millennia of lives lived and lost. Even the gods whom they depicted were mostly dead and gone, or else forgotten, their names become dust, their underworlds abandoned, their temples given over to ruin or wave.

Beyond the statues he sensed something stirring in the shadows, but held his tongue, for it was not his place to speak of it.

As the pilgrims filed in, Sleath watched their faces: one looked on in abject fear, another in awe, the third in quiet determination. Each of them had travelled here with hope in their hearts, to lay their broken lives before the reborn god, to seek her intervention. And each of them, he knew, would receive exactly the answer they required.

Amaranth stirred, rising from her seat. She looked resplendent in her pale, gauze-like gown, a spectre drifting into the light.

She looked down upon the three pilgrims and smiled, her eyes flicking back and forth as she studied their upturned faces. "Step forward," she said, beckoning to Nok. "You have come far and suffered greatly, and I would hear from you first of all."

Nok did as she was bid, coming to stand before the Queen. Hesitantly, she slid the burlap sack from her shoulder and placed it on the tiled floor between them. The contents rattled as they settled. "My brother," she said, her voice quavering. "He is…broken. My people—*I*—beg of you to fix him."

Amaranth smiled, not unkindly. "Why? Because he was not like others? Because he was lost?"

Nok nodded. "His body was rejected by the Greenwood. He could not be saved. He no longer exists in this realm."

Amaranth stepped down from the dais. She placed a hand upon Nok's shoulder. The wildling flinched but did not pull away. "Oh, but he *does*, Nok. He lives on in you. This you already know."

"Is that what happened at the Kith encampment?"

"Allow me to ask you this: is it not a virtue to be different? To stand apart from others and wear your freedom boldly, for all to see?"

Nok looked confused. "I'm not…Yes, I suppose it is."

"Now consider: what is a life without loss? How do you measure meaning if all you strive to do is persist? How do you know what it truly is to *live* if you cannot die?" Sleath searched Amaranth's face as she spoke, saw the sadness inherent in those words. "It is because you are broken that you are whole. You carry more with you than the bones of your dead."

Nok shook her head. "I don't understand."

"In time, you will." Amaranth brushed her finger lightly against the wildling's cheek. "But for now, your attentions are demanded elsewhere. As we speak, Utharat stirs the Kith to rise, anxious to reclaim his usurped underworld. The Wolkin stand in his way. You must return to your people and lead them through the hardship to come. Teach them of loss and the strength that might be found in it. Deprive the poison god his becoming."

Amaranth turned away from her then. Nok looked on, confused, hurt. "But—"

"Quiet now. I must speak with another."

She took a step towards the priest, who, lip trembling, fell to his knees before her. At one remove, the panicked scribe continued to scratch frantically in his journal.

"Rise now, Brother priest."

Ambrose slowly got to his feet. For perhaps the first time in the man's life, he looked utterly lost for words. "Lady Amaranth. I bring the blessings of my Order, and I most dearly welcome your return amongst the Pantheon. We are honoured to bask for a time in your magnificence, to raise our voices in songs of tribute. It is my solemn duty as Arch-Brother-Imperialis of the Upper Order of the Unanswered, that I would put to you a question—"

"No," said Amaranth.

Ambrose stuttered for a moment in disbelief. "No?"

"No," confirmed Amaranth, her tone firm but gentle. "I will not answer your question."

"Please, my Lady, I have travelled far to seek enlightenment."

"And so you shall continue your journey. For what is a priest who knows the whole of their god? It is in the search for enlightenment that you find your truth, not in easy answers. The journey *is* your faith. Waste not your years in song, or on your knees, but seek instead to *live*. For that is worship of the richest kind. That is tribute enough." She offered him a benevolent smile. "I bid you make haste to the continent of Khafristan, where an elder god seeks succour in madness amongst the Velinites. He must be returned to reason if he is to play his part in the coming war. Go to him, and draw him back to the light. Show him how to live again."

"*Me?*"

"Who better? Only he of silver tongue might coax Aedus from his fugue. And he *will* be needed in what comes after." Amaranth's gaze was unwavering as she studied the priest. "The road ahead of you is long, Brother Ambrose, and filled with hardship and suffering. How you choose to face such tests will be the making of you. Trust that *I* have faith in *you*."

Tears were running freely now down Ambrose's cheeks. "Thank you, my Lady," he said, his voice cracking. "I shall endeavour to live up to the challenge you have set."

"I do not doubt it," she said, turning towards the knight. "And now we face another test."

Pallor was grinding his jaw. Sweat beaded on his brow. Now that his time had come, he looked unsteady, uncertain. He stepped back, raising his sword. The tip hovered close to Amaranth's breast.

"I would challenge you, Lady Amaranth, to the death."

"You would lose," she said softly, stepping closer, so that the point of his sword tore at her dress, pressing lightly against her flesh. A single twist of his blade and he could finish her. But he did not.

"That, my dear Queen, is precisely the point."

Amaranth sighed. "Have you heard nothing of what I have spoken? Don't you understand? Death is not a beginning. It is an *end*. Tell me, what is a knight without a quest? Are you so ready for completion, to bring an end to your tale? To abandon all that you have wrought and render it meaningless. Is all of your work in this realm done?"

"But I am a Knight of Perish," said Pallor, his voice cracking. "It is my duty to seek an honourable death from a worthy foe, to undertake my journey through the underworld and seek rebirth. You, my Lady, of all here present, must surely understand."

"And then what?" said Amaranth. "When that is done. When you have trodden a circular path and you are back to where it all started. A lone knight, with no purpose but to die again. Over and over. To turn away from all who might love you, simply to fill a void in your own heart." She stepped back, and the tip of his sword faltered. "Consider, now, that there are more worthy quests to undertake, Sir Pallor. The balance of this world is shifting, and there is need of men such as you. I would grant you such a quest."

Pallor dipped his head in a bow. "Lady, you humble me." He lowered his sword.

"A new king sits upon the Briar Throne, but malevolent roses prick his throat. He has become enamoured by one who would twist his thoughts towards their own ends. Free him of this burden before it is too late—but mind, he will not thank you for it."

Pallor swallowed. "As you command."

"We are all here broken things," said Amaranth, "and that is my final blessing."

Sleath swallowed. His mouth was dry. *Now, it comes.*

Behind the throne the shadows erupted, bursting to life, like a murder of startled crows suddenly taking wing.

Amaranth staggered, her expression pained. She opened her mouth as if to speak, but dark blood welled from her parted lips, dribbling down her pale chin. A dark stain spread across the front of her dress like spilled ink.

Nok screamed, wrenching her blade from her belt, just as Ambrose staggered back, aghast, his jaw working but no sounds spilling out.

Pallor looked on, frozen, his sword trailing upon the flagstones. "Stonn?" he said, his voice a parched whisper. "What have you done?"

Sleath darted forward to catch the crumpling form of the god, moving with surprising grace given the mechanical rasp it provoked from his limbs. He lowered her gently to the floor, holding her head and shoulders in his arms.

Behind her, on the dais, stood Stonn, a glinting, bloody dagger in her hand. "I couldn't let her do it," she said, her face a storm of emotions. "I had to stop her. I'm sorry."

On the ground, Amaranth let out a burbling gasp.

"Go!" rasped Sleath, tears staining his cheeks. "Go, all of you! Remember this day well, and remember, too, her words. You know what you must do."

"I'm sorry," repeated Stonn, as she came to stand by Pallor's side.

Silently, they retreated—Nok and her brother, Ambrose and his scribe, Pallor and his squire—on towards whatever future they would help to shape. On, to whatever path the Broken Queen had set them on.

Amaranth waited until their footsteps had receded, and all in the room was once again quiet and still, save for the gentle sobbing of her servant. "All is well, Sleath," she said, her voice growing weak, so that he had to hold her closer to hear her breathless words. "Everything is as it should be. Now I, too, am a broken thing." She smiled once more, and it was beatific, pure. Her eyes fluttered. "Oh, and next time—I promise—we shall repair your legs."

She exhaled, and was still.

Sleath wiped his eyes with the back of his hand. "Next time," he said, cradling her close, "always bloody next time."

Acknowledgements

Many thanks to Marie O'Regan, who invited me to take part in her new venture and gave me the excuse I'd been looking for to delve into the troubled lands of Durstan. Thanks also to Peter and Nicky Crowther; to Cavan Scott; to Jose Duncan; and to Fiona, James and Emily for keeping me going with tea, cakes and banter.